COVENANT
WITH
THE BEAST

by
Robert R. Jones

COVENANT WITH THE BEAST
Robert R. Jones

ISBN 1-57558-014-4

Cover design by Danny Phillips.

Acknowledgments

I would like to thank the following people for their various contributions to this work:

Dr. Lynette Wert, Dr. Marie Saunders, and Dr. Bettie Jo Knight of the University of Central Oklahoma for their encouragement, suggestions, and support;

Irene Martin for helping plant the seeds that have grown into this book;

A. Fred Cole for knowledge and insights into the prophetic portions of Scripture;

Mary Anne Cole Jones—my bride, my friend, my greatest fan and most constructive critic—for keeping me on track.

Finally, all the honor and gratefulness of which I am capable goes to my God and Savior, Jesus of Nazareth. More than anything else, His inspiration has made this project what it is. My sincerest desire is that this work of fiction will serve to encourage many to covenant with the Messiah.

Table of Contents

Table of Contents continued . . . . .

Prologue: Petra, A.D. 2004

I really don't know where to begin. So much has happened. As I sit here with pen in hand, I am struck with awe by the primitive conditions in which I find myself. It is an absurd picture: Thomas W. Beckett, anchor for North America's top-rated news program, sitting in a cave in the Middle East with no camera and no computer, only a pen and paper to record my musings.

If someone had told me five years ago that I would lose my job, my family, my best friend, all within such a short time frame, I would no doubt have laughed out loud. I am not laughing now.

I take a certain pleasure in the beauty of this place. The high cliff walls and the multitude of small and large cave openings that dot the cliff faces and mark the entrances to people's homes lend Petra an air of majesty. However, the stark beauty of the cliffs serves only to emphasize the seriousness of our situation. We are all fugitives, some two thousand of us, I am told. Most of the people here are Israelis, though I have seen nearly every ethnic group imaginable in the few days since I arrived.

Since I arrived? No, since I was brought here. I have the jovial, balding Habib to thank for that. I owe him more than I will ever repay. He and his scouting party found me in the desert outside Jerusalem five short weeks ago. I was fleeing for my life and nearly dead from dehydration.

But I am getting ahead of myself. Habib wants me to write an account of where I came from and the circumstances that brought me to Petra. He says that we need a written sample of people's experiences and how they found a new life here. In this way we can encourage each other in these times of heavy persecution. "And besides," he says with a chuckle in his voice, "what else is there to do here but read and write?"

That is not entirely true, but beyond the necessities of daily life and the security details, there is not much in the way of entertainment. And I can understand how people who have made the sacrifices necessary to come here would want some encouragement from time to time.

Habib's request is an easy one for me to fill. I am a journalist. Reporting events is what I do. Now, though, instead of an instant audience, I will be recording this account for posterity's sake. But the time now is so short, I have to question the value of committing these things to paper. I will do it, though, because I could not restrain myself if I tried.

So here it is—my account of the events that led me to a new home, new friends, and a new life.

Chapter 1: The Colorado Rockies, A.D. 1999

The Colorado Rocky Mountains are idyllic in winter. The world there sleeps under a blanket of ethereal white. Or so I've heard.

The last time I was there, I was too busy fearing for my life to care. Our white Global News Network minivan skidded and slid up the curving mountain road as our News Director, Henry T. Wilson, Jr., struggled to get us to the assignment on time. I appreciated his intent, if not his methods. The cameraman, "Chip" Goya, had a look of intensity on his face that told me his thoughts and mine were running along the same lines: If we ever get out of this alive, we're going to kill Henry Wilson.

We arrived at the Colorado Rockies retreat thirty-seven minutes later. The retreat consisted of a dozen ground-hugging structures built from all local materials. The buildings blended in so well with the surrounding flora that had it not been for the single mountain road that brought us straight into the complex, Henry would never have found it.

As the van screeched to a halt, Henry turned around in his seat. A bright smile beamed from his chocolate-brown face. "We're here."

Chip groaned and held his stomach. I got out of my seat and opened the van's side door so hard that it bounced back when it reached the end of its track.

"Remind me never to ride with you again," I said, stepping out of the van.

Henry chuckled. "How you gettin' back, white boy?"

I took a deep breath before turning around to face my director and best friend. "I'm driving."

From somewhere in the van, I heard Chip's weak "Yes!"

After Chip threw up outside the van, he felt well enough to accompany Henry and me inside to register for the conference.

The receptionist at the front desk was a pale, middle-aged woman wearing a flowered dress and what had to be two to three pounds of cheap looking costume jewelry. Her red hair was unkempt and jutted out of her head in a way that suggested that even if she wanted to do anything with it, it would not have submitted.

She smiled broadly. "Welcome to the Moment of Global Unity Conference," she said. "You people are late; the prayer and meditation service starts in half an hour." Although she was chiding us, her smile

3

never showed the least hint of fading.

"We're with Global News Network," Henry offered.

The receptionist looked genuinely surprised for a moment and then stood and gasped in recognition. "Oh, the press," she said. "Ariel said you would be coming, but I didn't think there would be so many of you."

Chip looked around. "There are only three of us here, ma'am."

She covered her mouth and giggled. "No, not you three—Reuters, AP, CNN—they're all here." She bobbed her head from side to side. "No matter. The more the merrier, I always say."

I shot Henry a look of frustration. I hated being the last reporter to any event, even to one in which I placed as little credence as the Moment of Global Unity. Henry's shrug said what both of us knew to be true. It couldn't be helped. Linda Friedman had given us the assignment late, greeting us that morning with airline boarding passes.

GNN's Denver affiliate had the van ready when the plane landed, and, with the exception of Henry's driving, everything had gone off without a hint of trouble. Still, we were late.

A small, muscular, dark-skinned man with a long black ponytail stood beside the receptionist's desk. He had not been there moments before, and I wondered how he had made his entrance so stealthily.

"Eric will give you a tour of the complex," the receptionist said. "After that, he will show you to your meditation chambers, where you may rest and prepare for the meeting this afternoon." Then she smiled even wider. "It's going to be <u>wonderful</u>."

Eric led us through a large open room with concrete floors that served as the Conference Center. Display booths lined the walls and obstructed the path with a maze of multi-colored distractions. A gypsy sold incense and crystal balls next to a Hindi woman selling copies of Rama's <u>Encounter With Krishna</u> and the <u>Kama Sutra</u>. People of every imaginable shape and size crowded the too-narrow aisles.

Chip tried to take in every sight, sound, and smell. Henry nodded politely to the vendors and muttered "excuse me" when he wanted to get past someone.

Spying a set of Tarot cards, Chip laughed. "Hey, Tom," he said. "They've got a cure here for whatever ails you."

"At this point, I'd settle for a good dose of Dramamine. Between Henry's driving and all the incense these people burn, I'm about to throw up."

Chip reached up and slapped my shoulder. "Be my guest. Trust me, you'll feel better."

"Maybe I should buy you a crystal," Henry said. "You look like you could use some positive energy."

"Henry," I said, "have I ever told you you're an idiot?"

"Only a dozen times today, Thomas."

The meditation chambers were little more than ornately decorated wood framed paper walls. Each cubicle was about ten feet on each side and contained a rug, a set of candles, and a wash basin.

Henry whistled a long, low note. "Very Japanese," he said.

Eric gave a curt bow. "For the peace of your souls. May you find rest and contentment here." He did not wait for a reply, but turned and left. I realized that Henry and I were alone. "Where's Chip?"

Henry said, "He got sidetracked by that Korean booth—the one with the big yin-yang banner—said he'd catch up."

Really. "I didn't know he was so attracted to all this Eastern mysticism."

"He's not. But he is attracted to pretty little Korean women who like to talk about their Tao."

We freshened up as well as we could in the cramped accommodations, and Henry went to track down the leader of the Moment of Global Unity while I put on my camera makeup. Chip showed up long enough to say that he was going back out to the van to get the camera.

Miraculously, all three of us met at about the same time outside the main entrance to the largest of the buildings, the amphitheater. Dug into the ground, the amphitheater was essentially a huge semicircular hole with log steps, wood bench seating for five thousand, and a wood shingle roof that only extended over about half the seats. The stage and remainder of the seats were exposed to the mountain sky. This feature of the building made it necessary for all the participants to wear their heavy coats to the main event of the Global Unity Conference.

I knew from listening to the weather reports that this whole area of Colorado had been blanketed with two to three inches of snow earlier that day. Yet, every trace of the morning's snowfall had already been eradicated from the amphitheater. Well, at least they're not too infatuated with Nature, I mused as I descended the stairs.

Henry reached over my shoulder and pointed to a tall, thin woman on the stage. She was dressed in white flowing robes, and a floral headdress sat on her curly, jet black hair.

5

"That's the director of the conference," he said.

"That's Ariel?" I said, exaggerating the "Ah" sound.

Henry chuckled. "Yeah, her real name is Patricia Jamison. Very powerful lady around here. Don't mess with her."

"She can't be too powerful if she has to lie about her name."

"She doesn't, really. From what I can tell, Ariel is her spirit guide. People just call her that because she is so connected to him—her—it. Whatever."

"I see."

As we reached stage level, Ariel spread her arms wide and glided toward us. She was graceful in her movements and more beautiful than I had been prepared for. She had a wide face with cheeks high and smooth under eyes that were beacons of icy blue. She smiled peacefully. "Welcome to the Moment of Global Unity, Thomas Beckett."

I shot a questioning look at Henry, who tried his best to look innocent. Ariel stopped her advance mere inches in front of me and brought her arms around in a wide arc, placing a hand on either side of my face. She peered into my eyes; it felt as though my soul were being invaded.

Ariel knitted her brow as she saw . . . what? "You are deeply disturbed in your soul, Thomas Beckett. You seek rest for your mind."

"What? Now, wait a—"

"Fear not, Thomas Beckett, for you shall find here what you seek." She smiled and raised her arms in an expansive gesture. "Here, under Nature's watchful eye, we shall together seek unity and peace for our troubled world." She turned and glided away, leaving me bobbing in her wake.

"You all right?" I heard Henry say.

Forcibly shaking the heart-wrenching sensation the woman in white had induced, I muttered, "Yes. I'm fine."

Henry glanced at his watch. "Good, 'cause we got a segment to get in the can, and our satellite linkup is in a little less than thirty minutes."

If we missed our broadcast deadline, my segment would not make it on that night's show, and this whole trip would have been wasted. As every newscaster knows, "Old news is no news."

Chip readied his recording equipment—a combination audio/video laserdisc camera that weighed less than five pounds and was smaller than some of the old 8mm home movie cameras. The technology it employed was fairly new, but news departments all over the globe had come to depend on this particular camera for its light weight and rugged versatility. The self-contained design and satellite broadcast capability of this model had even allowed one GNN cameraman to record the events leading up to the airline crash that killed him along with eighty-seven other people last month. The cameraman sensed something was wrong with the airplane, so he grabbed his camera and burst into the cockpit, filming and commenting on the events as they transpired. Just before impact, he hit the SEND button, and GNN reported the story before the FAA investigators had even been called. The FAA cried foul until they recovered the camera with the laserdisc intact. From it they were able to attribute the crash to "pilot intoxication."

Chip signalled that he was ready. I collected my thoughts and cleared my throat. Henry looked at his watch and counted down from five.

"This is Thomas Beckett reporting from the Colorado Rocky Mountains Resort, which is playing host to this year's Moment of Global Unity.

"The air here is charged with a special excitement as the participants ready themselves to usher in the New Year. But this is no ordinary New Year's Eve party. Millennial fever has captured the hearts of those who have come here to say good-bye to the Twentieth Century and ring in the Twenty-first.

"Sponsored by the Ecumenical Society of North America and supported by no fewer than fifteen separate faiths and denominations, the Moment of Global Unity is the spiritual descendant of the Harmonic Convergence of ten years ago. Like the Harmonic Convergence, the Moment of Global Unity is a special time set aside for people from all faiths to come together for the purpose of meditating and praying for peace all over the world.

"And speaking of all over the world, this event has spread from the heart of this continent to other regions across the globe. This group and half a dozen others in other countries will, at midnight Greenwich Mean Time, all pray for the peace of our small planet.

"We at GNN wish them success. For Global News Tonight, I'm Thomas Beckett."

I smiled for a moment until the red light on Chip's camera went out.

"Chip, you get everything?" Henry said. Chip nodded as he fiddled with his camera.

"Well, then, that's a wrap," Henry said.

7

I let out the breath I had not realized I had been holding. Henry placed a big, beefy hand on my shoulder.

"Pretty good for a cold run, Archbishop," he said. From the day I introduced myself to the tall, stocky African-American named Henry Wilson, he had taken great pleasure in playing on the joke afforded by the historical names of Thomas Beckett and Henry II. In the weeks following Henry's promotion to News Director, the joke had spread to other members of the crew, and quotes from the 1967 film starring Peter O'Toole and Richard Chamberlain abounded.

"Thank you, my Prince," I replied.

"You know, Thomas, when I was growing up in Queens, I never dreamed a white man would ever call a black man 'my Prince.' Man, I love this job." Henry turned and walked away, laughing.

As Henry's laughing faded, eerie music swelled from hidden loudspeakers. A spotlight appeared on the stage. Ariel stood in the center of the spotlight with her arms extended upward. She held her face skyward in a pose that suggested the soaring flight of an ecstatic eagle. Curious, I sat down.

The exotic music reached a crescendo and stopped. Ariel lowered her arms slowly, the wide sleeves of her robe completing the allegory of flight. She looked out over the audience. Seated on the front row, I noticed the faraway look in the Priestess's eyes, as if she were listening to something in the distance and straining to hear.

The amphitheater grew deathly quiet. Even the normal rustling and chirping of forest animals was strangely absent.

When Ariel spoke, her voice was a soothing, singsong monotone. "Uncounted millennia ago, the dust around a small, unimportant star collected to form this planet we call earth. Through millions of years, life arose out of the primordial pits of ooze.

"The force of evolution has brought us to this place—a people, a race of beings at odds with Nature. For too long, we, the pinnacle of evolution, have worked to destroy the thing from which we arose. We have resisted Nature, refusing to live in harmony with her."

A small group of Buddhists to my right were nodding. Ariel spread her arms wide.

"But we have good news for you tonight—that is all coming to an end, my friends. Today, people across the globe are joining together as we are here to unite their minds and souls as one, and at twelve midnight Greenwich Mean Time—the very beginning of the twenty-first century, we will all visualize peace. We will make it happen.

"The spiritual energy of the world is more focussed today than it has ever been in the history of humankind. We have reached the Nexus, the turning point in the history of our race. We are ready to take the next step forward."

Ariel looked about and brought her hands together in a gesture of supplication.

<u>What next step?</u> Judging by the rapt involvement of the audience, I seemed to be the only one with that question. Even Colorado's Archbishop, Reginald James, nodded from his front row seat in placid agreement with every word Ariel spoke.

She continued, "We as a race are destined to take the next step in our perfection as children of the light. The time is now, this year. I feel the stirrings in the spirit realm. The spirits are calling us to perfection. They are calling us to take our rightful place in the Universe."

She paused. Her face became shadowed with emotion. She was in pain—anguish. Ariel's face contorted horribly, and tears poured forth.

Surveying the room, I noticed most of the audience was crying as well. Inexplicably, I felt a lump rise in my throat and forcibly swallowed. <u>Idiot. What's wrong with you, Thomas? This is silly. Why all this emotion?</u>

"But there are those," she said, her voice no longer the soothing monotone, now broken and harsh, "who will not take that next step. They will resist the call of the spirits to their dying breath. They are arrogant, intolerant, and inflexible. Captive to their own narrow-mindedness, they will not accept other belief systems or see the truth in all religions. They refuse to take the next momentous leap in their evolution.

"We will evolve; we will change," she said, regaining her composure. "We will continue in harmony with Mother Earth, but not so for the others. Soon, they will be carried off to a world where they will be allowed to develop at their own pace. They will not hold us back from our destiny any more. In a moment's time, in a mere heartbeat, they will disappear."

In defiance of all logic, I knew deep within that at least part of what she said was true. I could not explain it, but somehow I could sense that major changes were in the offing. Something big was about to happen to Mother Earth. But people disappearing—taken away to another planet where they could develop at their own pace? That was too much. For the next week and a half, I grinned every time I thought about Ariel and her spooky-spiritual speech.

Still, there was that small part of my brain that would not allow me to bury the experience. Ariel's speech played in a loop in a dusty corner of my subconscious for several weeks, like a wise fly that buzzes around your head but always stays out of sight.

Looking back on it now, I think that discomfort was what drove me to take the first week of vacation time I had taken in over four years— a decision which subjected me to some good-natured ribbing at the hands of Henry Wilson. He seemed to feel it was wrong of me to only take time off during leap years, when everyone else had to work an extra day. I smiled sweetly and told him where he was welcome to spend his extra day this year.

Colorado's natural beauty had reminded me of my sister's peaceful acreage in Tennessee, so I decided to take Ann up on her standing offer of a soft bed, a warm fire, and a few home-cooked meals.

Chapter 2: Tennessee—February, A.D. 2000

My flight touched down at 10:05 a.m. on Monday the 28th, and Ann was there at the gate with Bill and the boys when I walked off the plane. Ann was wearing a lavender flowered dress, and her smile beamed across the waiting area as she ran to greet me. I dropped my two carry-on bags to receive her hug.

"Oh, Tom, it's good to see you."

"Hello, Annie. It's been too long."

Ann pulled away from me. She had tears in her eyes.

"Yes, it has," she said without judgment.

The Reverend William Randolph Reece ambled over to us with his sons right behind. He flashed that abominable ear-to-ear preacher's grin of his and extended a hand. I shook it and discovered his grip was as firm as ever.

"How are you, Thomas? It's good to see you."

"Bill." I had never cared much for the man my sister had chosen to be her husband. Just then I remembered why. He was a preacher all the way from his swept-back hair down to his spit-shined cowboy boots. Even when he was silent, he oozed sermons. I forced a smile and muttered something about how much I appreciated them all coming to the airport to pick me up.

In spite of my feelings for the man, I kept a strict policy of silence. I would never belittle him in front of my sister. She loved him greatly—that much was apparent. Ann had been so happy since she married the man whose parishioners affectionately referred to as "Pastor Bill."

I had never understood the abrupt change in little Annie's outlook that had gone hand-in-hand with her and Pastor Bill's courtship. I was concerned about the subjective, touchy-feely religion Pastor Bill instilled in my sister. He had changed her somehow, and I hated him for it.

I could see Ann's inevitable fall from the faith barreling down on her from behind like a subway train in a darkened tunnel. I knew it would happen. A random disaster would strike their family, as disaster always does in a random world, and she would be crushed. She would hate God for not being there and herself for being duped. She would grow to become a bitter old woman. And it would be his fault.

As a loving brother, I wanted to let her down gently, to cushion the impact of her impending disillusionment. I had told her gravely and repeatedly during our frequent phone conversations that religion makes people unhappy, not happy. The perky Ann would hear none of it. I could almost feel her smile sadly over the miles as she would say, "Someday you'll understand."

Bill drove their minivan, and Ann turned the front passenger seat toward me so we could talk. As we were leaving the airport, Ann apologized for the heavy traffic. I chuckled and told her that in New York, if you could see any pavement at all, traffic was light.

Ann's laugh made her blue eyes sparkle and her blond curls quiver in the ray of sunlight that streamed in through the windshield. She was grayer than the last time we saw each other, and there were a few more wrinkles when she smiled, but she <u>projected</u> beauty—a quality I was at a loss to understand. It was more sensed than seen, as if her face only served as a framework for something infinitely more profound shining out from behind.

"Oh, I almost forgot," she said. "Thomas, do you mind if we stop at a grocery store before we go home? I haven't been into town to shop since you called to tell us you were coming."

"No, of course not. Look, Ann, I'm sorry if the notice was too short—"

"Not at all. It's just that we've . . ." Her voice trailed off and she and Bill shared untold joys and sorrows with a brief meeting of the eyes. "We've been busy."

I made a mental note to pry more information out of her later.

We had stopped at an intersection, and when the light turned green, Ann placed a hand on Bill's arm.

"No, wait," she said.

Bill did not move. The minivan did not move. The vehicle next to us, a small import, ventured into the intersection. We still did not move. It seemed we sat there for an eternity with the car behind us sounding its horn. Then the rest happened all at once.

A red streak and a panicked screech of tires from the left materialized as a sports car plowing into the import that had beaten us into the intersection. The red car struck the import just behind the driver's door, folding it in half and pushing it several yards before the two cars—now merged into one unrecognizable heap—came to rest just outside the intersection.

Bill put the minivan into Park and opened his door, but Ann's and my feet hit the ground first. I went with Ann to check on the driver of the import first, while Bill ran to the driver of the sports car. I hated Bill even more for that. He was a fool. Who cares about the fate of the person who caused the accident? What about the innocent victim?

This particular innocent victim, a teenage girl, was most assuredly dead. Blood matted her hair and covered the shattered side window where her head had impacted. Blood also coated the dash and steering wheel, and her head rested on her shoulder at an impossible angle that could only mean a broken neck.

I walked around the import, leaving Ann and her sons with the dead woman. Bill was helping the driver of the sports car out of his smashed vehicle.

<u>This is just perfect</u>, I thought. <u>Once again, the innocent pay for the stupidity of the irresponsible</u>. This is just the sort of senseless tragedy I knew would usher in the downfall of Ann's faith. But I knew this incident would not trigger the disillusionment—it would have to be something closer to home. Perhaps I could make her see that during my visit. Maybe then she would give up her religious games.

I strode toward Bill and the criminal driver fully intending to make him pay for what he did. Death would be too merciful for him, I decided. He deserved prolonged pain. First I would show him what he did, and then I would make certain the victim's family had a chance to confront him.

What I saw next stopped me in mid-stride. Bill was praying with the man.

That was when I became convinced the good pastor had gone over the edge. Rage welled up in me, and all I could think of doing was punching both of them.

The odd thing was, all I could do was think about it. I had literally stopped in mid-stride and could not move. I could move my head and my mouth, but no sound came out. My feet, it seemed, had become part of the asphalt. It was as if some outside force were holding me back. It might have been a witch's spell, if I believed in such things.

Then Bill, the insane pastor, laughed and hugged the man, and the spell was broken. I almost fell for lack of balance. I turned to complain to Ann about her idiot husband in time to see her comforting the bloodied driver of the import. The woman I had been convinced on first glance was dead was instead very much alive and feeling quite well.

I have heard that trauma is like that. Megadoses of adrenaline and endorphins make their way into the blood stream, and people do not realize right away, sometimes even for hours, how much damage they have sustained. Often by that time, it is too late.

Sirens heralded the arrival of the police and an ambulance, and soon I was back in the Reece's minivan with Ann and her family.

Bill and Ann seemed strangely overjoyed by the near-tragic accident. As they giggled and cried and shouted "Hallelujah" and "Thank you, Jesus," and other such nonsense, I tried to piece together exactly what had happened.

First, Ann told Bill to wait at a green light. Why? A superstitious person would say she had a premonition, perhaps would even call her psychic or clairvoyant. But I am not superstitious, and my sister is not clairvoyant. She was doubtless acting on a random impulse that just happened to coincide with a sports car running a red light. Pure coincidence.

Then there was the teenager with the apparent broken neck. Had I misjudged her appearance that much? Impossible. I've seen enough dead bodies to know what one looks like. Yet, minutes after the accident, she was coherent and walking. She must not have been as bad as she looked. I must be slipping.

So by the time we reached the grocery store, I had convinced myself that what I had seen was no more than a collection of random events that on the surface had the appearance of—dare I say it—miracles. That, at least, was how I knew Ann and Bill would interpret these events.

I decided not to broach the subject of the accident with Ann. If her world-view demanded that she see such things as divinely ordered, I would not argue. Philosophy and Theology I would discuss with her, but I would never discount one of her "obvious miracles." Because miracles are from God, and far be it from Thomas Beckett to argue with God.

The rest of the day was given over to settling in on my part while Ann worked with her sons on their school lessons. I admired her commitment to home school her children. She had been at it now for nearly six years, and her reward was great—Brent and Robbie consistently tested in the top ten percent of every standardized test they took.

Mercifully, Pastor Bill spent much of the day in his study, praying and studying and preparing next Sunday's sermon. Except for a few muffled shouts and unintelligible gibberish, I did not hear from the man until dinner time.

After dinner and four hands of Canasta, it was time for the boys to retire, and they went to their rooms without argument. The good pastor went to pray with them, and Ann and I were left alone to clean the kitchen.

"Tom," she said as she loaded plates into the dishwasher, "what did you think about what happened this morning."

"This morning?" I decided to be coy. I had promised myself I would not broach the subject.

"You know, the accident."

"Oh." Well, there it was, out in the open, up for discussion. The dishes were my only witness that I did not bring it up.

Ann put her hands on her hips and studied me. I tried not to make eye contact. I still did not know how to tell her that what happened today was in no way miraculous.

"You don't believe a miracle happened today, do you?"

"No, I don't."

"Sit down."

"I beg your pardon?"

"Listen, Mister Investigative Reporter, you have managed to talk yourself out of the truth. We are going to sit down and review the facts so you can get your story straight." As she was talking, my baby sister pushed me back into the dining room and onto a chair. She sat down across from me.

"First of all," she began, "I stopped Bill from driving out into that intersection. Why do you think I would do such a thing?"

"Pure chance. Maybe you saw something out of the corner of your eye."

"No. That was a blind intersection. The overpass blocks the view to the left for anything more than a few yards. Or hadn't you noticed?"

That stung. I had noticed but was unwilling to admit that none of us could have seen that car coming.

"Maybe you heard the car—perhaps on some subliminal level," I countered.

"That sports car was one of the new electric models. They are practically silent."

I knew she was right. But how to explain what happened?

"Tom, this is what I have been telling you about all these years. God's Spirit lives within me. He lives in Bill and in the boys, too. God spoke to me at that intersection this morning. It wasn't an audible voice; it was something inside. He told me we shouldn't go when the light turned green. That's why I put my hand on Bill's arm."

"You're telling me you're psychic."

15

"No. I'm telling you God loves me, and He takes care of me and my family. And in the times we're living in, that is critical."

"Listen, Ann—"

"No, you listen, Thomas Beckett. You don't want to believe I heard from God? That's fine. Let's look at the rest of the facts. That teenager in the other car was dead. She had no pulse."

"Then my initial impression was correct." Images of a blood-stained car interior flashed through my memory. Then I saw her walking around, alert and coherent.

"She was dead, and now she's alive," Ann said, leaning forward.

"Oh, please, Ann. Are you going to tell me you have the power to raise the dead?" This was going too far.

"I don't, but God does. Do you remember when we were children, Tom? You were in Mrs. McNash's Sunday School class, and I would always tag along. I was too young for the class, but I always said I was too scared to be alone, remember?"

I smiled. "Yes. I would be so annoyed with you, and Mrs. McNash would say, 'Tommy, appreciate your sister now. You two won't always be together.'"

"And do you remember Mrs. McNash's favorite book of the Bible?"

"The Gospel of John."

"Good. Then maybe you'll remember this verse: 'Verily, verily, I say unto you, He that believeth on me, the works that I do shall he do also; and greater works than these shall he do; because I go unto my Father.'"

"I remember." But I did not like the direction this conversation was taking.

"Tom, all I'm saying is that God's Spirit lives inside me. I didn't raise that girl up—He did."

I stared at the wall and clenched my teeth for a few seconds to keep myself from saying something I might regret. Ann waited patiently, and the sound of the grandfather clock ticking in the living room was like the sound of a time bomb counting off the final seconds before the explosion. I had the uncomfortable sensation that time was running out for me. If Ann was right about what had happened—that the teenage girl had been raised from the dead—then she was also right about a number of other things.

Impossible.

"Ann," I said, finally, "I'm not going to argue with you. If you choose to believe that what happened today was a miracle, that's fine with me. However, you should know that if I choose not to believe it, that is my right as well."

Ann's eyes glistened and the tip of her nose reddened, and a single tear found its way halfway down her face before she wiped it away with an angry gesture.

"You're a stubborn man, Thomas Beckett. I used to think you would come around some day, but now . . ." Ann turned her head toward the window to try to regain her composure.

"But now, what?"

She steeled herself and turned to face me again. "The clock is running down. The time of God's mercy is almost up. Tom, if the miracles you saw today won't turn your heart, you could not even bear to see some of the other things Bill and I have seen over the past several months. The Church of Jesus Christ is more powerful now than it has ever been. We are in the middle of the greatest move of God's Spirit this world has ever seen, the final revival before the Lord returns. I know it. I can sense it in my spirit. If you don't accept Jesus now, it may be too late."

Visions of the priestess Ariel invaded my mind. She also had spoken of major changes in the "spirit realm." Coincidence? Probably. Religious charlatans would always need the occasional spiritual crisis to keep their customers coming back for more.

But there was something different about my sister's spirituality. While Ariel had feelings and impressions, Ann had convictions. A part of me wished fervently that I could believe in Ann's Jesus. But I could not believe in a good and loving God—not with all the pain and suffering I had seen.

Life, I decided, must be much simpler for Ann than it is for me.

"The choice is up to you, Tom," she said. "You can either call Him Lord now and give Him the power to decide the course of the rest of your life, or you can wait until you stand before His throne, when He will have the power to decide your fate whether you want Him to or not. Either way, your knee will bow and you will confess that Jesus is Lord."

I remained silent. This particular conversation was obviously at an end.

Bill walked in and announced that Lance and Teresa would be stopping by tomorrow for lunch and to talk about their salvation experiences. Ann was beaming. I asked who Lance and Teresa were.

Bill said, "They're two new Christians. I invited them over for lunch so I could begin discipling them."

"Oh." I shot Ann a quizzical glance.

"Tom, they're the two drivers from the accident this morning."

I spent the remainder of my visit to Tennessee trying to decide why those two particular people were not in a hospital.

After I left the surreal religious world of my sister and her family, my life returned to normal. In fact, it was better than normal for a while. For a reporter, social, military, and political upheavals mean big business.

With the recent ratification of the World Constitution, the nations of the world had come under the governance of ten regional districts which began with the European Community and NAFTA. Each district was led by a prime minister or a president or a king who was a member of the World Cabinet. These individuals met on a frequent basis to discuss trade, food distribution, and other issues of global concern.

Officially, the World Cabinet members each carried equal influence—one person, one vote. Practically, though, this type of arrangement has never worked. History teaches us that in virtually any government, there will arise one who is regarded as the leader. Even if he is only a figurehead, it seems that humans have an innate desire to look at one person's face and say, "God save the King." So I suppose the same was inevitable with the World Cabinet.

The man whose name the reader has already supplied as Joshua ben-David was born Joshua Cohen to Israeli parents, and he was educated at Oxford. Beyond that, his origins are shrouded in mystery. He rose out of the obscure position of Finance Minister for the European Common Market to become within a few months the most powerful man alive.

In the opening days of the new millennium, no one suspected how deeply the lives of everyone on earth would be affected by this man and his meteoric rise to power.

Chapter 3: New York—September, A.D. 2000

I remember vividly the news report that changed my life, although at the time I did not realize it.

Worldwide political tensions seemed to be at an unprecedented high. Each night there was another war to report more violent than the last, usually between small countries and centering around an issue of ethnicity or land. I became so wrapped up in my work that I missed my sister Ann's weekly phone call and then neglected to call her back.

Then, one evening, we topped the news hour with something completely different.

Following the introductory theme music and greetings to our audience by my co-anchor and myself, I said to camera one, "The world today is in perplexity at the sudden and unexplained disappearance of hundreds of thousands, possibly even millions, of men, women, and children. This morning, at 5:53 Eastern Standard Time, something as yet unexplained happened. We have been getting reports all day from all over the globe regarding missing persons. We have been able to narrow the time of the event down from various eyewitness reports of people who were with a person or persons at the exact moment they disappeared.

"Most describe a flash of light; some say they merely blinked and their companion was gone. Earlier, I spoke with New York City's mayor, Don Richardson, who was an eyewitness to this event."

The monitor cut to a close-up of a dark, round face crowned by short, mostly gray hair. The normally vibrant Richardson was on the verge of tears.

"I was in the bathroom tying my tie, and Nell had asked me a question, but I didn't quite hear her, so I went into the bedroom. She was . . . she was sitting on the edge of the bed, looking so beautiful—" The tears that had been building up just behind the veil of the mayor's self control burst forth. He inhaled sharply. "She looked up suddenly, like she had heard something, and then there was this flash of light—" Another deep breath. "And she was gone. Just like that. All that was left on the bed was her night gown."

The camera cut back to me and I said, "Many people worldwide have had similar experiences. This is certainly a tragedy of global proportions. More about this when we return."

When the final count was in, nearly two billion men, women, and children—fully one-third of the earth's population—had been a part of what came to be known as the "Great Disappearance." Industry, especially North American industry, ground to a virtual halt. Chaos reigned supreme as skeleton-crewed police departments scrambled to maintain control of rioters, looters, and the panic-stricken.

In the ensuing months, hospitals abruptly understaffed and over-run with patients became breeding grounds for all sorts of diseases. New epidemics cut a swath through the patient populations at most of them, causing more panic and rioting. Rural American towns, which had in that one day an average reduction in population of about 80 percent, became ghost towns for a brief moment.

But nature abhors a vacuum, and abandoned buildings are no exception. Soon criminals fleeing from the law and each other found refuge in the abandoned houses and stores. Small town America was destined to become a war zone, a place where no law enforcement officer would venture.

On the whole, the Great Disappearance seemed far removed from and unrelated to the world of Thomas Beckett. Aside from the night janitor and a sound engineer who never again came to work, no one I worked with was directly affected by this event, or if any of them were, they failed to mention it. It was only after the war that I discovered that I <u>had</u> been affected by the Great Disappearance in a very personal way, but as it is with all impending tragedies, I was that day blithely unaware that within two weeks my life would take a turn for the worse.

Even though I felt personally unaffected by the Great Disappear-ance, I was keenly aware as a reporter that an added bit of turmoil had been stirred into the soup of world politics. This event, catastrophic though it was, was probably not by itself enough to ignite the flames of the next war between the world's superpowers. Chaos is a wonderful incentive for war but is rarely the reason for it. Things might have continued for planet earth on a rather normal course but for the work of a team of Israeli archaeologists and historians.

The excitement of the nation of Israel over the re-discovery of the ancient Ark of the Covenant was matched in intensity by the fear and ire of its Arab neighbors. All of the peace negotiations of the eighties and nineties went out the proverbial window as violence and threats of jihad filled the air. Within days, a coalition of Arab nations formed for the express purpose of taking Jerusalem by force. Not content to face the mythological wrath of the Hebrew Ark alone, the Arabs enlisted the help of their allies to the north.

The temptation was there—a world in strife is ripe for conquest. The Russian bear awoke.

Chapter 4: The War for Jerusalem

We had a difficult time gaining flight clearance from the Israeli government, but our news director in Tel Aviv knew some people, and the pilot, camera operator, and I were soon on our way. By the time our white-and-blue GNN helicopter landed just outside the old city of Jerusalem, the Russian army was within fifty miles of the Israeli border, well on its way to joining the assembled Arab armies for the battle of the decade.

People have often asked me if going into dangerous situations ever made me reconsider my career choice. I always told them that boring days when the best news story was a political scandal were what made me think about a different job. The truth is that I loved the excitement of a dangerous assignment almost as much as I did the prestige of being North America's top-rated news anchor.

Yet, as we flew over this land over which so many had fought for so long, I had to wonder if this was going to be the "big one"—the final, decisive battle for control of the Middle East. And if so, did I really want to be in the middle of it? I forced myself not to think in those terms. My instinct for self-preservation was definitely becoming stronger with age.

The Israeli Defense Forces were ready for battle, and dozens of fighter jets streaked overhead. The first shot had not yet been fired in the hope that the frantically-organized peace negotiations in Rome would succeed. I knew they would fail. The nation of Israel had bargained away all its defense capabilities gradually over the past twenty years, and she was now a juicy, defenseless steak on the plate of world events. Add to that the fact that Israel's traditional allies to the west were making no offer of military support, and the end of the Hebrew nation seemed imminent.

The Israelis had been powerless to do anything but watch as the advancing armies rumbled across Palestinian-occupied territories, cheered on as heroes by the inhabitants of the West Bank and the Golan Heights.

Upon hearing of the advance, the Israeli Prime Minister went into cardiac arrest and was pronounced dead on the scene. Chaos reigned in the Knesset. Israel was suddenly without a leader. Rather, the tiny nation found itself with too many leaders at once.

By the time what was left of the nearly-dismantled Israeli military was called into action, the Russian and Arab armies had surrounded Jerusalem. All of the Arab-Israeli peace treaties of the past twenty years evaporated in a puff of diesel and jet fumes as the Russo-Arab armies held thousands of guns to the head of their hostage Israel. It was a war that was not yet a war, as a tenuous cease-fire crackled in air that had yet to see any smoke spout from the muzzles of weapons.

The reaction of the West had been truly appalling. I had read the wire services reports on the peace negotiations in Rome. North America bowed out due to domestic and economic difficulties, and United Europe failed to see any consideration beyond Russia's economic motivations. European diplomats communicated frantically with Moscow, trying to barter oil for peace. They had no concept of what this war was about. Their failure was assured.

This war was not about oil or political position; it was about religion. I had seen this same scenario played out time and again to varying degrees during my three decades of news reporting. Two groups claim a divine right to a parcel of land, regardless of its intrinsic worth, and the resulting war kills hundreds, or thousands, or millions of zealots and innocents alike. We call them "holy wars," though there is never anything holy about them. For this reason, among others, I abhorred religion. Humankind's plethora of hypocritical philosophies had caused more death and destruction than any other reason ever thought of for war.

Now I was witnessing the culmination of aeons of religious conflict, and the result of this conflict would change the balance of power for the planet. It was a winner-takes-all contest, and the free world was taking a coffee break.

For the Muslim nations, this was the mother of all holy wars, the final conflict in a centuries-long struggle between them and their sworn enemies. The Russians naturally wanted to gain control of as much liquid buried treasure as they could, but staving off their greed would never stop the war.

The Hebrew Ark had been found. The war would happen as surely as if God had decreed it.

I found out later that He had.

I wore a Kevlar helmet and flak vest over my light blue shirt as I stood on the Temple Mount with my back to the sealed Eastern Gate. The morning sun baked the back of my neck, and I sweated from more than the heat.

Normally, I smiled at the camera as the final seconds were counted down to air time, but not today. Instead, I furrowed my brow and pressed the small earpiece farther into my left ear in order to hear co-anchor Wendy Matherly's audio cue from the "Global News Tonight" studio in New York. Between the planes flying overhead and the noise of the crowd around me, I was having difficulty hearing anything.

Israeli soldiers scurried about as officers barked orders. One of the soldiers, a kid in his late teens, not paying attention to where he was going, ran into me, and I staggered backward two steps before regaining my balance. The soldier muttered his apology and hurried on.

The camera operator, whom I had never met before, seemed on the edge of a mental breakdown as his eyes skittered between his equipment and the drama unfolding on the mountains outside the city gates.

I thought ruefully about the posthumous Pulitzer they would no doubt award me for my courage in reporting the opus of the upcoming massacre. My hands were shaking. I took a deep breath. "Beckett, you're a regular Edward R. Murrow," I said to no one in particular.

"Here it comes, Mr. Beckett," the camera operator said. I reflexively glanced over my shoulder expecting to see an incoming rocket before I realized the man was talking about my audio cue.

I cupped my hand over my ear in time to hear Wendy's voice say, "And now, with a live report from the Temple Mount in Jerusalem, here is Thomas Beckett. Thomas?"

I dropped my hand and looked into the camera lens. "Thank you, Wendy. I'm standing in front of the Eastern Gate just a few hundred feet from the Dome of the Rock Mosque in the old city of Jerusalem. We are watching the culmination of a series of events that threaten to end the life of the tiny nation of Israel.

"Arab, Israeli, and European leaders are right now attempting a last-ditch effort at peace as dozens of armies await the command to descend on this city and reclaim it for Allah. Less than a mile around me in all directions, the largest combined armed force the world has ever seen is now gathered to bring an end to what was begun here in 1948, when Israel regained her homeland after nearly 2,000 years of political exile. Now, Wendy, it looks like the Muslims are finally going to succeed in their jihad."

Through my earpiece, I heard Wendy's thin voice ask the prearranged question. "Thomas, what made the Arabs choose an all-out war?"

"As you know, Wendy," I continued, "over a month and a half ago, Rabbi Aaron Dyan and his colleagues with the New Levitical Order uncovered what they believe to be the Ark of the Covenant, a religious relic that has not been seen since the reign of Solomon. They now claim to have done all the ritual cleansing necessary to reinstate the Ark as the focal point of Hebrew worship. All that remains is to rebuild the Temple that stood on this very mountain until the year 70 C.E., when the Roman army destroyed it.

"The Arabs are afraid, perhaps justifiably, that with the discovery of this relic of ancient Judaism the Israelis will wish to regain complete control of all the lands they have given to the Palestinian Arabs during the past two decades in various peace treaties. Since Jerusalem is also home to the Dome of the Rock Mosque, the third holiest shrine in the Islamic world, the Arabs fear that they stand to lose access to this holy site, even though the new Temple would be built in direct line with the Eastern Gate behind me, and the Dome of the Rock would remain untouched."

I glanced over my shoulder as an Israeli fighter jet streaked by, leaving in its wake a deafening roar. I shuddered visibly and felt blood drain from my face. "It looks like this time, the Arabs may get what they want. I'll stay here and bring you live reports for as long as I am . . . able. Live—for the moment, at least—from the Temple Mount, I'm Thomas Beckett."

Machine gun fire echoed in the distance.

"Come on," I said to the camera operator, "let's find some cover." A tank's main gun fired some two hundred yards outside the city. The gathered crowd in the Temple area, military and media people alike, ducked as one giant single-celled organism. Then the organism shattered, and individual people ran in every direction.

I dashed for the stairway that would take me down to the relative safety of the Wailing Wall, and the ground beneath my feet moved. At first it seemed an explosion had rocked the city, but the motion continued and even increased in intensity.

Someone yelled, "Earthquake!"

Gunfire, tank guns, airplanes, and exploding missiles filled the air with a persistent roar that threatened to knock me off my feet. People crowded the stairways and jammed themselves into the Dome of the Rock until there was a line outside.

I found myself alone with the noise a few yards from the tiny shrine called the Dome of the Tablets. I dashed toward the mosque, stumbling as the stones under my feet bucked and rolled. A large rock rose and tripped me, and I fell to my hands and knees as a fighter jet careened out of control and exploded on the Mount of Olives. I imagined

I heard the pilot scream.

A wrenching metallic sound followed by the loud popping of cracking concrete emanated from the Dome of the Rock, and I watched in horror as the huge gold dome shifted and fell in slow motion, crushing everyone in the building. The remainder of the structure then crumbled to dust, imploding on itself. I cursed myself for letting the camera operator get away.

The explosions of weaponry increased in intensity on the other side of the city walls, continuing for miles around. I had a moment of lucid thought through my terror. The city of Jerusalem ought to have been leveled by now, but other than the havoc the earthquake was wreaking, the city still stood. <u>Why aren't we all dead?</u> I thought.

I could not answer that question. The world was shaking. Shock waves tossed me about like a jellyfish in stormy seas. The universe was in utter disarray. Chaos had replaced the Cosmos. I thought I heard a scream and then realized it came from me. I covered my ears, but my hands were unequal to the task of shutting out the sounds that were larger than I. They penetrated every molecule of my body. I sought order, but there was none. I was Chicken Little. The sky was falling.

Several minutes or several hours later—time has little meaning when every second is an eternity—when the ground beneath me felt solid again and explosions had ceased pummeling my body with their concussions, I got to my feet and walked on shaking legs toward the Eastern Gate. The wall of rock that had for hundreds of years cut off access to and from that portion of the Temple Mount still stood. I was stunned that an earthquake that could level the Dome of the Rock and make solid ground seem like a rowboat in the wake of an ocean liner somehow failed to affect that wall. But I had no time to ponder such things. I had to get out of the city and see what had happened.

When I finally made my way out of the city, I was dumbstruck. The only movement I saw was in the smoky distance, where a few scattered groups of soldiers still fought each other. Other than that, every tank, vehicle, and body was still.

I walked onto the quiescent battlefield. Bodies lay everywhere. Many were burned beyond identification, but most wore distinctive uniforms—Russian, Syrian, Libyan, Ethiopian, and several others.

And the blood.

It covered the ground in what appeared to be one huge pool. All the bodies, even the burned ones, bled profusely. I watched the rising tide of crimson as it swept toward me and surrounded my shoes.

Instinctively, I jumped back, but with no effect. The viscous red substance flowed faster toward me, as if alive. I succumbed to a wave of vomiting that threatened to throw my entire body into the muck. I staggered forward three steps before regaining my balance. I resigned myself to the continually rising filth and surveyed the landscape.

Dead and dying men covered the ground as far as I could see. The Mount of Olives showed no green save for the uniforms of the soldiers, no brown save for the skin of some of the dead men. Red dominated the mountain, covering it from top to bottom in a horrible cascade. It appeared as though every fallen man had been struck in the carotid artery and bled to death. The flow seemed eternal. The macabre tide rose still farther and began to fill the Kidron valley. Russian tanks in the lowest portion of the valley became buried to the tops of their treads.

The combined armies of the Russian and Arab nations had all at once turned on each other, and total annihilation was the result. Exactly why this had happened, I decided, was a question best answered by historians and philosophers.

I became vaguely aware of a rising shout from behind Jerusalem's wall. Surveying the scene one final time, I breathed deeply from the death-soaked air and turned back to the Old City. I had to find that camera operator.

What happened following that bizarre battle could only be characterized as a religious revival for the nation of Israel. As they saw it, their God had saved them from their enemies and was once again smiling on His chosen people. I found it difficult to argue with their reasoning.

The celebration lasted for days. The Levitical priests began referring to this event as "Ezekiel's War" for reasons that escaped me until I interviewed the High Priest. He read to me from the latter portions of the Book of Ezekiel a passage that, had I not consulted a Gideon Bible upon returning to my hotel, I would have believed had been written after the fact.

I remember my skepticism well. Israel's enemies destroyed by God in this battle were called Gog, Rosh, Meshech, Tubal, and other names of regions and tribes no modern person would recognize. Sensing my disbelief, the High Priest retrieved an orthodox commentary on the historical significance of those names. It all added up to a Russo-Arab alliance coming from the north to attack Israel, only to be defeated by a supernatural act of God. The logic was inescapable. Why else would a coalition of armies suddenly turn on itself to the point of total destruction? Maybe their God had saved them, after all.

Soon, however, it became apparent that Israel needed help of a more physical nature. True, their enemies had been defeated, but their economy was a train wreck and their land was a mess.

That help came in the form of a charismatic leader named Joshua Cohen.

Joshua Cohen had already risen to preeminence as United Europe's Finance Minister after less than ten years of service. This stunning success was traceable to his ingenious restructuring of the global banking system after the Great Disappearance had destabilized the industries and financial institutions of many of the world's countries. Ezekiel's War provided Joshua Cohen with yet another opportunity to capitalize on his position and skill.

With the total defeat of the Russian military, Europe staged a financial coup. Two days after the war, the United Europe Council voted unanimously to manage Russian and Arab finances, and by extension, their governments. As Finance Minister, Joshua Cohen was named provisional leader of Russia and its allied Arab nations.

Then, without the advice of the European Council, Cohen signed the Covenant of New Jerusalem, a seven-year treaty with Israel on behalf of United Europe, Russia, and the Arab states. In a televised ceremony that is still replayed every year on the anniversary of the signing, Joshua Cohen declared himself King Joshua ben-David, Protector of the Nation of Israel, King of Jerusalem, and Prime Minister of Europe, Russia, and the Middle East.

Israel's borders were redrawn, massive loans came from the European Community to help the recovery process, and the Jewish priests began searching their scrolls and drawing up plans for the next Temple.

Chapter 5: After the War

My ears were still ringing when I returned home two days after the war. My flight was delayed, and the late edition news was already off the air by the time I opened the door to my apartment. After dropping my luggage by the coat rack, I scuffled into the kitchen and poured myself a glass of Chablis. Sitting in my favorite chair, I reviewed the notes I had made to myself prior to my departure.

Between the grocery list and the reminder to pick up my dry cleaning, there was a note to call Ann. She had left a message on my recorder shortly before my trip to Israel—it was the day before the Great Disappearance story—and I had called her back and left a message on her recorder. I hated playing "phone tag," but Ann and I usually missed each other a few times before we finally got together for our weekly talk. I finished my glass of wine and resolved to call her in the morning.

Morning came. I called and her answering machine picked up. After the beep, I dutifully left a message. "Hello, Ann, this is Thomas. Just returning your call from last week. Call when you can—I'll be home by ten." I hung up the phone, and on a whim replayed Ann's message.

"Tom, call me as soon as you can. I hope you're not out of town or anything. I can't wait to tell you what's been going on here. God is on the move like never before." She almost squealed the next sentence. "It's _so_ exciting! Hurry, call fast."

I smiled. Little Annie. She sounded even more chipper on the recording than she had during my visit. So proud of her religion and her preacher husband and their two squeaky-clean boys. After all these years, she still took great pleasure in telling me how I needed Jesus in my life.

Remembering my recent visit to the Reece household, I picked up the picture of Ann and her family that I kept next to the telephone. It was a two-year-old photo, but it was the most recent one I had of her. I silently kicked myself for leaving without getting a new picture.

Ann and Bill were sitting on a tree stump somewhere in the Tennessee woods, with ten-year-old Brent and eight-year-old Robbie posed on the ground before them. Bill and the boys wore flannel shirts and jeans, and Ann wore jeans with her favorite sweater, a thick navy blue pullover that did a nice job of complementing her blond hair and hazel eyes. They were all smiling.

As I left for work that day, I did not realize that the recording on the machine and the picture beside it were all I had left of Ann and her family.

I spent the following year or so in turmoil, drinking too much and spending too much time and money confirming what I already knew to be true. Ann and her family were gone forever.

The Great Disappearance had hit home.

I steadfastly refused to accept any of the offhand explanations given by various authorities for the Great Disappearance. Regardless of what the Priestess Ariel said in her frequent infomercials, my sister had not been abducted by aliens who took her to a different planet where she could evolve at her own pace. Neither had she been wiped out, phased out, nor dematerialized by an earth that was weary of her narrow-mindedness. I did not know what had happened; I only knew there were no pat answers.

For another two and a half years following the stupidity of my drinking binge, I buried myself in my work. There was certainly plenty of it. The only problem with doing that is that one's co-workers become one's family, and as with all families, there are some relatives you just can't stand.

Chapter 6: New York, March, A.D. 2004

The "Global News Tonight" stage lights, like old friends, warmed my face as I sat behind the long table that had almost become a part of who I was. I adjusted my tie, and the makeup artist tapped my nose with a powder puff. The copy boy had placed my script neatly in front of my seat, just where I liked it.

I quickly leafed through the pages to ensure that they were all in the right order and that none of them had been turned backwards or upside down. After nearly ten years as a Global News Network reporter and anchor, I really did not need a script—I practically memorized copy as I wrote it—but some of the staff took a wicked pleasure in making occasional "mistakes" in an effort to embarrass me on-camera by causing me to stumble over a word or make a sour face.

And there it was. Page five, the earthquake in Japan story, upside down. I righted the page and made a mental note to speak to Linda Friedman about the juvenile behavior of the staff.

"Global News Tonight" co-anchor Wendy Matherly walked behind the desk and sat down beside me. Though it grated me, I looked up and smiled. She was wearing a navy skirt and bright red blazer with navy lapels and big navy buttons. I always hated to see her wear that particular blazer. The fire red color looked good on her five-foot ten frame, and it matched her personality, but it played havoc with the cameras. I am certain she knew it, too. She either did not care about imposing on the crew, or she enjoyed making them work harder than they had to.

"Good evening, Thomas."

"Good evening, Wendy." I sniffed the air as Wendy studied her script. "You're wearing new perfume?"

She shuffled her papers, ignoring me. "Where is that story?"

"What story?"

"You know, the Detroit massacre. Oh, where is it? Those copy boys are such screw-ups." She slammed the papers down on the desk and glared at me. I almost laughed. Some women, like my ex-wife, are good at showing anger. Wendy Matherly was not. She always looked like a sunburned Barbie doll.

The basso profunda voice of Henry Wilson, Jr. came over the intercom. "Two minutes to air."

I smiled sweetly. "That's my story, remember?"

Wendy cursed. "I don't believe it. That was my story, you cretin. I took that call."

"And then you left. Some other big story, as I recall." I studied my fingernails in an effort to look nonchalant. "By the way, what happened to that big lead of yours?"

"Shut up, you pig. Lou was going to write the Detroit story for me—you knew that. You stole my story."

"I didn't steal it. It was given to me."

"What?"

This was getting good. I had earned this moment of revenge and was enjoying it. "When Linda found out that you had gotten that call and then just left, she stormed out into the middle of the newsroom and yelled, 'Would someone please tell me why any responsible journalist would walk out of the newsroom when she's got a story to write?' Nobody said a word. Then she looked at me and said, 'Beckett, get the Detroit branch back on the phone and get the facts. That ought to keep Blondie on her toes.'"

"You're lying."

I met her eyes. "Matter of policy. I don't lie." Actually, I had. Linda never made that comment about keeping Blondie on her toes. But at the time, I felt it was a nice touch, since Wendy despised being called Blondie. It made her feminist blood boil.

"One minute to air," came the disembodied voice. "And Thomas, quit tormenting your co-anchor. We want a happy Barbie doll for the program."

"Yes, my Prince," I said.

"Male chauvinist pig," Wendy groused to the air. There were chuckles from behind the cameras. Wendy stared at me for a long moment. I pretended not to notice, focussing my attention instead on the papers in front of me.

"As for you," she said, "you'll get what's coming to you."

"O.K., people," said tall, youthful Assistant Director Kaitlin Murray, "We're on the air in ten, nine, eight, seven, six . . ."

The "Global News Tonight" theme music played. Wendy and I collected ourselves and smiled at Kaitlin as she counted down the final five seconds on her fingers. The red light on camera one lit, and the show was on.

"Good evening, everyone, I'm Thomas Beckett."

"And I'm Wendy Matherly."

"And this is Global News Tonight. At the top of the news, the leaders from nine of the earth's ten regions met today in Rome, where they will discuss many issues of world concern, such as radioactive fallout in Russia, disaster relief for the United States' earthquake-ridden west coast, and the latest in a rash of new diseases coming from the lowering waters of the Nile."

The camera moved slightly to my left, and the viewing audience saw at mock 3-D image of China's red flag appear over my shoulder.

"Of primary concern to the World Cabinet will be the arms buildup in China. As the leader of the only earth region not yet to ratify the World Constitution, Chinese Emperor Huong Chouw Peng has sent waves of rumor rippling through the waters of world politics by not attending the summit."

A montage of high-definition satellite photos replaced the flag over my shoulder. They showed various military scenes, tanks and troops parading, missiles firing, and fighter planes taking off.

"The World Intelligence Organization reports that military activity is on the rise in China, and they speculate that if the Asian giant's activities are not curtailed, within five years they will have an army to rival any on the face of the earth. Wendy?"

Wendy's camera light switched on.

"Thank you, Thomas." She managed to shoot me an icy glance as she smiled and turned to face the camera. She did that often, and I hated it. Mostly because, having seen numerous tapes of the show, I knew that look was lost to the cameras. To the world, she was pretty, competent Wendy Matherly—no one watching the show would ever know what a conniving, vindictive person she was.

I let myself get so caught up in my thoughts that I nearly missed my cue. A slight flush overtook my face, and I was not sure if it came from anger or embarrassment. "And now," I said to the camera, "a tragic note. An earthquake measuring 8.5 on the Richter scale struck the Japanese city of Kyoto this afternoon, making this one of the largest earthquakes ever recorded. An estimated 80,000 people remain buried under the rubble in the third natural disaster to hit the island nation since 1995. The main tremor caused damage as far away as Osaka and was felt in the town of Taira, nearly three hundred miles away.

"Red Cross and United World Relief workers are on their way to Japan now with food, water, and medicine for the people of Kyoto and the surrounding towns. However, officials expect rescue efforts will be delayed as workers contend with the after-shocks of this major earthquake."

As I cued the commercial break, I had to fight down a sudden lump in my throat. Once the camera was off, I placed a hand over my mouth and cleared my throat.

<u>What is wrong with me</u>? I thought. <u>I'm Thomas Beckett, news anchor. I don't get emotional about the news. A group of people died half a world away. What is that to me</u>? My vision blurred and I blinked a hot tear onto my hand. I glanced up in humiliation at Kaitlin Murray.

"Thomas, what is your problem?" she said, placing her hands on her hips.

Without a word, the makeup artist was at my side, hovering over me like a hummingbird at a flower. I concentrated on maintaining control of this sudden and unwelcome well of emotions. "I don't know, Kate," I said.

Wendy looked over at me and stuck out her bottom lip. "What's wrong, Pookey?" she said. "Big, tough man can't take a little bad news?"

"Shut up, Wendy."

The rest of the show that night was a battle between my emotions and my intellect. I had no easy answer to the question of why I was reacting this way, but deep in the center of all that I was, there was an ache, a throbbing emptiness that I hoped would go away on its own. I convinced myself that it would, eventually. But until that happened, I would have to suppress it, to control it, just as I had all the other negatives in my life.

Chapter 7: Morning

The telephone woke me at 10 a.m. I felt a rush of adrenaline until I realized that it was Saturday. I stumbled over a pair of shoes on the way to the phone, cursing all the way.

"What?"

"Yo, Pop." said the Brooklyn-bred voice.

I rubbed my free hand through the tousled pepper-gray mess that hours before had been finely coiffed hair. "Anthony? Is that you?" I said, blinking the sleep away.

"Yeah, Pop, it's me, Tony. Hey, you comin' to get me, or what?"

I shook my head to clear the cobwebs.

"Get you?"

The teenager snorted. "Yeah, get me. It's our one-weekend-a-month weekend, remembah?"

The adrenaline rush returned. I took a deep breath and began to feel coherent. Anthony. One weekend a month. Right. "Well, of course I remember, son," I lied. "I just overslept. I'll be there in an hour, all right?"

"Yeah, sure, Pop."

I don't know if I can stand to listen to that insipid accent of his all weekend. When I married Carol, a native of Brooklyn, I had been so infatuated with her I stupidly felt I could overlook the terrible way she spoke. As the son of an American officer and a British nurse, I had always prided myself on having a definitive, cultured accent. It was one of the reasons "Global News Tonight" captured two-thirds of the domestic market. I had planned to teach our children to speak in a way that would make them successful, as I had been.

I remember coming home from work late at night and sneaking into the nursery to check on my new son. He always seemed so peaceful and still. I would look at that tiny baby and marvel at the incredible potential that he represented. I knew he would grow to be someone great and influential. I would give him the key to success by training him to be a great public speaker. With those speaking skills he could be a lawyer, politician, or possibly a lecturer. Whatever path he chose, he would rise to the top of his field because he was a Beckett.

But ever since the divorce, Carol's influence with Anthony had been too strong. Now I could barely tolerate a conversation with my own son.

<u>I have to keep us busy somehow . . .</u> "Tell you what, son, I'll make it up to you—we can go to the zoo."

"The zoo? You want to take me to the zoo?"

"What's wrong with the zoo?"

"Pop, I'm seventeen years old."

I clenched my jaw and felt the beginnings of a throbbing headache. This was too much. "That sounds like a personal problem to me."

"Zoos are lame."

"Fine. We don't have to go to the zoo; it was just a suggestion."

"Yeah, well suggest something better next time."

I suppressed a surge of rage. <u>This is my son I am talking to. This is also the person I'll be spending the next two days with. I should try harder to get along.</u> "So, Anthony, how is your mother?"

"Hey, yo," Tony said, "You can cut the small talk, all right? I ain't a kid. Besides, I know you don't really care about Ma anyway."

I said nothing.

"So, I guess I'll see you in an hour," Tony said and hung up.

"I coulda taken a cab myself, y'know. Shoulda told me the Benz was in the shop."

I took my eyes off the cab driver's wildly bobbing dreadlocks to look at Anthony. The cab made a hard right turn that sent me lurching toward my son. I caught myself before I landed in his lap.

"Whoa," he said, "nice save."

I pounded my fist on the bulletproof plexiglass that separated us from the reggae-loving cabbie.

The cabbie made an abrupt lane change to get around a trash truck before cocking his head sideways. "Ya, mon?" he said.

"Would you mind slowing down? We'd like to live to eat lunch."

"Okay, mon, but it goin' ta cost you more." The man grinned in the rear-view mirror.

I caught a glimpse of Anthony in my peripheral vision. Was he smiling, enjoying his father's predicament? Anger rose to my neck. "What do you mean, cost me more? It's the same distance no matter how fast you go."

"Ah," the cabbie said, "but it take more of my time to slow down. Time is money, you know."

I pointed at the meter in the center of the dash. "That measures mileage, you cretin. You can't charge me for your precious time."

The cab lurched into a tight left turn, throwing me into the passenger side door.

"I don' care what dat ting measure. You goin' to have to pay me money to slow down, mon."

"All right, you win," I said, fishing my debit card out of my pocket. I waved it at the driver. "Fifty dollars if you slow down now."

"Sound good to me," the driver said as he braked to a complete stop.

"Wait—why are you stopping?"

The cabbie laughed. "Because we here, mon."

My apartment building stood placidly outside the cab's window. I had truly been taken for a ride. Now Anthony was laughing, too. Reading the total on the screen, I whispered a curse. The driver had already added his fifty dollar tip. I grumbled about the cab driver's business practices and inserted my debit card into the reader. When the machine beeped its approval, I retrieved the card and opened the door.

"Let's go, Anthony, before this gentleman charges us for any more of his time."

The lights in my apartment came on automatically when I opened the door. Anthony followed me in, looking around the room, and set his duffel bag down by the bathroom door.

I was glad to be home again. I despised the untidiness of Carol's first-floor apartment, even though I had not been invited in and only stood at the door. The hundreds of "collectibles" she always kept made her home look constantly cluttered. When we were married, it became so distracting that I found I could not think. My home, on the other hand, was a masterpiece of simplicity and utility.

My sixteenth-floor apartment occupied barely seven hundred square feet, but most of it was open. The kitchen was only partially separated from the living room by a low bar, and two doors on adjacent walls of the living room led to the bathroom and the bedroom. The wall opposite the front door housed a large picture window, through which the hawkeyed observer might see on a clear day the old, abandoned United Nations building.

The United Nations were no more, the World Cabinet having taken over from its offices in Rome following the ratification of the World Constitution. The ensuing Wall Street stock market crash had merely been the final push New York City needed to make its spiral decay into filth, despair, and poverty irreversible. I silently thanked the Fates that my income depended not on North America's economy, which had never fully recovered from the Great Disappearance. GNN's worldwide market determined the popularity and job security of one Thomas Beckett.

Anthony's voice shocked me out of my reverie.

"You never rearrange your furniture, do you?"

I set my keys on the hall table by the phone and unbuttoned my jacket. I remembered Carol's penchant for rearranging things and pitied Anthony. She had always had a compulsive need for change that, among other things she did, nearly drove me insane.

"No, Anthony, I don't fix things that aren't broken."

"Pop, would you stop already with the 'Anthony' stuff? It's Tony, see—" He grabbed my cheeks and squeezed in rhythm with his speech. "To-ny. To-ny."

I shook my face free with an angry snap. Anthony backed up a step and raked the hair out of his eyes. Two generations of the Beckett family stared at each other for a tense moment.

I broke the silence. "Your name is Anthony."

"But I want to be called Tony. It's what Ma calls me, what my friends call me, cousins, everybody. Except you."

Now red-faced with anger, I stepped toward my son and spoke in a menacingly low tone of voice. "You want to know why I call you Anthony? It's because a name like Anthony Ian Beckett spells success. You can go anywhere, be anything you want with that name. Like anything else, you have to want it. You have to apply yourself and work toward your goals, but if you burden yourself with a low-class nickname like Tony, you'll never be anything more than a greaseball."

"So, what—I'm a greaseball, now?"

Oops. "Anthony, wait. That's not what I—"

"Not what you meant, huh? Right. People only say what they mean unless they're lying to get out of trouble. Look at you—always so careful and controlled, so perfect. What's it gotten you? You live alone, see your family once a month, and the only friends you have are at work. You've never been a dad to me, so don't try to teach me nothin'. And don't act like you did me any favors when you named me. It don't change nothin'. I'm still a bastard, just like you."

"Anthony!"

"Yeah, Ma told me about that night in the back room of her uncle's store. You never wanted me to know. Why, Pop? That was probably the only out-of-control thing you ever did." Anthony laughed bitterly. "You know, it's kinda funny. Here I've spent my whole life knowing I could never live up to your perfection. Then I find out the only reason I'm even alive is because you're not as perfect as you think you are. You made a mistake, and you're gonna make sure I pay for it for the rest of my life. You've always been ashamed of me."

"No, Anthony, I—"

"Don't even try to lie. You're no good at it. You're a fake, and I can see right through you."

Anthony grabbed his duffel off the floor and marched to the door. He flung the door open and turned to face me. I stared at him, mouth agape.

"You know, Pop, I may be a greaseball, but you're the loser." Then he was gone.

I stood frozen in shock. I was immediately furious with Carol for telling our son of his genesis and of mine. She had no right.

When I regained my senses, I ran down the hall to the elevators but was too late to catch him there. I caught the next elevator and burst through the revolving door just in time to see the back of Anthony's head through the window of a cab as it sped into traffic.

Abandoning the temptation to hail another cab and say, "Follow that car," I trudged back to my apartment and slumped down into the recliner, hoping my son would be all right. After all, at seventeen Anthony was practically a man. I decided to call Anthony later to make sure he made it home.

Chapter 8: The Preacher

As I readied myself for work Monday morning, I could not get my mind off Anthony and our unsuccessful weekend. Once the boy returned home, Carol called and gave me lecture number 347 about how I needed to be more of a father to Tony. My explanation of how unreasonable our son had been fell on deaf ears.

Apparently, so had my request to have my Mercedes-Benz 970SEL repaired by Monday morning. The mechanic had been more surly than usual when I called. He told me he had found something else wrong with the car. Typical. When I told him that the car had no problems when I had brought it in other than the rough idle I had asked him to fix, the mechanic unleashed a string of profanity so foul I thought for a moment I was back in Tel Aviv at the Arab-Israeli Peace Accord of 1999.

I hung up on him.

Then I repeated some of that same profanity under my breath as I crossed the street toward the subway station down the block from my apartment building. Muttering to myself, I would not have even looked up from the moving patch of concrete in front of me had it not been for the large number of people who were crowding past and heading away from the subway station.

I turned around to see where they were going and saw a young man, thin, with dark skin, black hair and a beard, standing on the hood of the police car that had been burned in a recent fire fight with some of the local gang members. A crowd was gathered around the man, and I could tell he was speaking but could not hear what he was saying. Like nearly all the people around me, though, I seemed to be drawn toward the man. I looked down at my feet before I realized that I had turned and started walking toward this strange person.

As I got closer, I noticed something else about the speaker. He seemed to be standing in a spotlight. I surveyed the area, trying to pinpoint where there might be a hidden spotlight, but saw nothing. Now close enough to hear the man's speech, I discerned that the mysterious light did not cast a shadow—it came from the man himself. I stopped cold.

The man was <u>glowing</u>.

I instinctively reached into my suit coat pocket for my PocketCam, a mass-market video camera that was no larger than a debit card and only slightly thicker. In all of my years as a reporter, this tiny device had been the best thing I had ever owned for on-the-spot reporting.

Using something called "nanotechnology," a term I sincerely hoped I would never be required to understand, the PocketCam had a tiny lens on one side of its flat surface. The lens focussed automatically and sent all the action through the processor to be stored digitally on a chip the size of my thumbnail. The PocketCam owner's manual stated that "no more than one-hundred minutes of video should be taken before emptying the stored data onto an optical storage device such as a laser disc or magnetic media." The other side consisted of a high-resolution LCD viewfinder.

I pressed the red button on the upper right-hand edge of the PocketCam and used the viewfinder to zoom in on the luminescent man. Was I seeing one of those auras that I had heard the Priestess Ariel and so many other New Age teachers talk about on television? Perhaps the video would provide some answers. I focussed my attention on what the man was saying.

"Listen to me, everyone," he said. "Time has run out. The Day of the Lord is here, and His wrath is about to be poured out on the whole earth."

There were discontented murmurs from the outer fringes of the crowd, but most of the people in front of me listened with a range of emotions from mild curiosity to undisguised rage.

"Repent," he continued, "and be baptized into the Lord Jesus, for once that Day comes, no one will be able to stand. Listen to me while you can, because I must leave soon, and you will be on your own, without light and without God in the world. Flee from the Day of Wrath. It is upon you."

A woman screamed, and I swung the PocketCam in the direction of the sound. A large man wearing dark glasses and a long scar down the right side of his face had produced a submachine gun from his leather jacket and levelled it at the speaker. In the heartbeat before anyone reacted, the gunman fired at the preacher.

I fell on my side as people all around panicked and ran. The gunman sprayed the crowd with flesh-ripping flechette darts from the muzzle of the weapon, and several screams of pain were followed by the dull crumpling sound of limp bodies hitting the pavement. I tried my best to look dead as four different people stepped on me in their haste to get away. A woman in high heels, a bright green coat, and too much makeup tripped over my legs. She fell to the ground, and her eyes met mine.

"Don't move," I said. "He'll think you're dead."

She stared at me in glassy-eyed horror as she struggled to get back on her feet, stabbing my thigh with one of her heels. The sole of that shoe did not touch ground again. The woman's back arched as two of the deadly darts struck her, sending her to the same spot of concrete she had just left.

I met her eyes again, seeing only the empty stare of death. Her foot rested on my thigh. I suppressed a shudder and waited for the gunfire to stop.

When I was certain it was safe to move, I slid my leg away from the dead woman's foot and sat up. The gunman was gone, running down the sidewalk. A police car flew by, sirens blaring. It screeched to a halt a few feet behind the gunman, and the officer on the passenger's side of the car yelled "Halt, police!"

The man levelled his weapon at the officer. The police officer opened fire, placing five rounds in the gunman's chest. He spun and fell face first on the sidewalk.

"So much for prison overcrowding," I muttered. My thoughts then turned back to the preacher. Was his body among the dozen or so lifeless forms lying in what seemed to be one large pool of blood?

I stood and was shocked to see the man that had been a point-blank target moments ago kneeling over one of the victims, a woman in her late forties. He was crying as he turned his face heavenward, his lips moving silently. He sighed deeply and stood.

I thought he was going to just walk away, but he reached down, took the woman's hand and said, "In the name of Yeshua of Nazareth, I say to you: Get up!"

I might have laughed out loud, but the woman's chest heaved skyward with a giant gasp, and her eyes opened. The preacher helped the woman to her feet and hugged her, the bloodied blouse soiling his shirt.

Mentally kicking myself for my lapse in journalistic integrity, I remembered the PocketCam. Bending down to retrieve it, I realized it was hopeless. There was a small dot of pavement showing through the camera's newly acquired hole.

"I'm telling you, Linda, I know what I saw," I said. "Global News Tonight" producer Linda Friedman leaned back even farther in her leather desk chair and steepled her fingers. Her long, drawn face usually went unadorned except for a frame of straight brown hair parted in the middle. The only element of this middle-aged woman's appearance I had ever been attracted to was the absence of wrinkles around her eyes. But that was because she never smiled.

"Tom, you know how this works." She sounded like a work-weary mother reminding her teenage son to take out the garbage. "No video, no story. All we were able to download from your ex-camera was a few seconds of some wacko yelling at people from the hood of a burned-out Ford."

I placed both hands on Linda's desk and leaned forward. "This guy raised twelve people from the dead. And I don't care what that camera did or did not show—he glowed. This is news. You have to let me do this story on tonight's show."

Linda Friedman stood and duplicated my stance, bringing our faces to within inches of each other.

"I produce 'Global News Tonight.' I don't have to do anything. As for your so-called story, you're welcome to put it on the wire services and the BBSs and see if anyone picks it up."

I stared down at the desk and clenched my jaw. I knew the smell of defeat. If, as the news anchor on the nation's highest-rated newscast, I could not air my own eye-witness account of what happened, then no one would touch the story, no matter how good it was.

I could place it anonymously on the BBSs, but the first respectable journalist who decided to follow up on the story would make the name Thomas Beckett infamous. That is, provided anyone did pick up the story amidst all the reports of global disasters that had become so prevalent, like the gigantic swarm of carnivorous locusts that was now ripping across Europe, or the many different wars that constantly raged in different parts of the world as petty dictators struggled to wrest control from the World Cabinet.

But the thought that remained foremost in my mind was: why was Linda killing this story? Before I realized my mouth had opened, I gave voice to the question. "All right, Linda, fine. You're killing my story. Why?"

Linda released her grip on the desk and picked up a cigarette from the pack by her left hand. Her eyes narrowed as she lit the cigarette and took a long draw. She exhaled a large cloud of blue smoke that followed her as she abruptly sat back down.

"Thomas, you don't have a story. Why don't you try the National Enquirer?" Then she laughed, still without smiling.

I drummed my fingers on my desk. The Enquirer. Now I know

what motivates all those disgruntled postal workers. I mentally began to play different scenarios that all had a common goal—how to get back at Linda Friedman. Several of them were too impractical, like simply shooting her or poisoning her coffee. Too sloppy. And I did not really want to face the consequences of such an act. It was just a thought. Others were too juvenile, like planting a virus in her computer or sticking bubble gum on the seat of her desk chair.

But more than revenge, I wanted answers. I touched a combination of keys on the keypad of my desk computer and was rewarded with a screen listing every story Linda had killed over the past twelve months, along with the first sentence of the story and Linda's official reason for canning it. For the most part, her reasons were logical—not enough air time, too little human interest, too local, etc. It was the large number of stories for which she gave no reason that caught my attention.

As producer of "Global News Tonight," Linda had the right to refuse to run any story she deemed unfit for broadcast, for whatever reason. She was not even required to give a reason, but being the meticulous person that she was, she nearly always did.

I marked the stories and downloaded them into my own database. I looked for the common element that would link all the stories and would make sense of Linda's actions. I did not search long.

Every story killed without reason over the past six months centered around a bizarre, supernatural event: sick and injured people miraculously healed, people raised from the dead, food and water inexplicably appearing for disaster victims, and on and on. Although some of the reports were sketchy, most of them gave credit for the miracles to an unnamed young man of Middle Eastern origin, often describing in detail someone very much like the preacher I had seen.

Checking the dates of the stories, I realized that there had to be more than one of these miracle-workers roaming around. No matter how impressive he is, a man just cannot be in Bogota, Damascus, London, Beijing, and New York City all in the same day. And those were just the stories submitted by GNN affiliates over the past twenty-four hours.

I scanned the list and murmured, "There must be thousands of these men. And Linda has buried every single one of their stories." I decided to confront her and sent a partial list of stories to the printer. A wry smile caught the side of my mouth as I congratulated myself on my investigative skills.

Linda Friedman seemed unmoved by my revelation. She barely glanced at the computer printout before leaning back in her overstuffed chair and steepling her fingers. "Do you have a problem with the way I run things, Thomas?"

"I have a problem with standing by and doing nothing while you kill every single story about these miracle-workers that comes across your desk. Linda, some of these stories are good, and most have video of some kind."

Linda leaned forward in her chair and narrowed her eyes. "Do you think all that matters to me? Don't kid yourself, Beckett, it doesn't. You want to know something else? You're the most arrogant, pompous idiot I've ever met. You and your journalistic integrity." Linda looked as though she might spit. "That's not what this place is all about. We're not here to hold a mirror up to Mother Earth so she can see what she looks like; we're here to keep her entertained and pacified so she doesn't start acting as ugly as she looks."

Linda looked around on her desk. Spotting the packet of cigarettes, she grabbed it savagely and flung two of the white cylinders onto the desk. She muttered a curse and picked one of the cigarettes up. She brought it to her mouth as if to light it, then thought better of that and put it down.

She continued, "You think I'm cynical, don't you, Thomas? Well, you're right, I am. I look around and I see a huge wasteland of humanity—nobody's any good. The best we can do is keep them glued to the tube night and day so maybe they won't get out and hurt someone.

"But these preachers you're talking about—they're dangerous. They stir people up, cause riots. Did you listen to what your man said? These guys talk about Jesus Christ like he was still alive and coming back tomorrow to conquer the earth and send everyone to hell. Can't you see how reporting stories like that would cause panic and dissention?"

I stopped pacing and studied my fingernails. I had always prided myself on my ability to work with nearly anyone under nearly any circumstances. But this issue loomed like an impending storm cloud. My producer and I were at an impasse.

"No, Linda, I don't see that," I said, finally.

"Then you're even more blind than I thought."

Chapter 9: Black Knight

"Good evening, everyone. I'm Thomas Beckett."

"And I'm Wendy Matherly."

"And this is 'Global News Tonight.' Before we begin, we have for you a late-breaking story. Astronomers at Kit Peak observatory verified today that there is a meteor streaking toward the earth. Using data provided by the Kit Peak scientists, GNN's own Dr. Ronald Sadler says the big rock will impact somewhere in the Atlantic Ocean." The studio monitor cut from me to the set next door, which was a mock-up of the GNN newsroom. Noticing how clean, uncluttered, and organized the desks were, and how calmly the paid extras carried out their mock duties, I suddenly wished I worked there.

Dr. Sadler stood in the foreground wearing a white shirt with the sleeves rolled up part way and a thin red-and-blue tie that hung loosely around his long crooked neck. As he squinted in the direction of the camera, I wondered why GNN's resident science guru had never invested in laser surgery to fix his eyes. <u>Maybe Ron just likes being seen as the nutty professor type. Why else would anyone choose to wear those plastic-framed bottlecaps?</u>

He glanced down at his script and wiped the sweat from his forehead before speaking. "The meteor that was spotted today, dubbed 'Black Knight' by its discoverer, will impact the earth in the Atlantic Ocean, anywhere from 300 to 500 miles off the coast of Ireland. It, uh . . ." He paused to look at the script again.

The edge of the paper quivered uncontrollably.

The thin man took a deep, shuddering breath and looked at the camera. "It's a big one," he said.

"Just how big is it, Dr. Sadler?" Wendy had spoken up before I could form the words. She was showboating—stealing glory from the star. I shot her a dirty look, but she was too intent on the video monitor to notice.

"Wendy, from what we're able to tell, the meteor is nearly fifteen miles in diameter with an estimated mass of over twenty-seven million metric tons. This will be the biggest meteorite ever to enter earth's atmosphere."

I laughed nervously and said, "Dr. Sadler, those numbers sound a bit intimidating, but you said the meteorite will strike in the Atlantic Ocean. Am I right in thinking we really have nothing to worry about?"

"Thomas, we are running computer simulated scenarios now to predict the effects on the global climate from this event, but we really won't know anything definite until the spectral analyses are in from the various observatories tracking Black Knight. Right now, I don't know what the meteor is composed of, and that will greatly affect how much damage it will do on impact."

"Well, how much time do we have?"

Ron Sadler took his glasses off and stared into the distance. Just when I thought perhaps Ron had not heard the question, the thin scientist looked squarely at the camera and said, "Three days. The meteorite will strike the earth in three days."

I lost my professionalism. "What do you mean, three days? Where did this thing come from? Why didn't we know sooner?" Kaitlin Murray waved her arms up and down, frantically trying to get me to settle down. I ignored her.

Ron Sadler sighed. "We would have known about it sooner, but Black Knight came at us on a trajectory that kept the sun between it and the earth. I have a model here—let me show you." Dr. Sadler walked a few feet to a model of the solar system that sat on a desk. Tiny motorized planets moved slowly around a florescent sun. Dr. Sadler picked up a pointer that had a small brown ball on the end. He held it up for the camera.

"This represents Black Knight. It came from somewhere on the outskirts of our solar system, from what is known as the Oort cloud. Um, that's essentially a large collection of rocks that orbit the sun out beyond Pluto. At some point, perhaps millions or even billions of years ago, Black Knight was bumped out of its orbit and began its journey toward the inner solar system on a flat arc that exactly matched the earth's orbit around the sun." Dr. Sadler moved the pointer around the mock sun in concert with the orbit of the tiny earth. Bringing it close to the sun, he changed its direction, moving it directly toward the third planet.

He continued, "The sun's gravitational pull yanked the meteor off course, accelerating it toward us. Even then, we didn't see it due to the glare of the sun. It has been about three months since Black Knight passed the sun. The only reason we know about it now is because the astronomers at Kit Peak were conducting research on sun spots when they saw an oddly-shaped spot in some of their photos. Lasers were then used to pinpoint its location and velocity."

The red light on camera one lit and I instinctively regained my composure.

"Thank you for that report, Dr. Sadler. Stay tuned, America. King Joshua ben-David returns to Jerusalem. That story and more when we come back." Camera two pulled back for a long shot of Wendy and me as the "Global News Tonight" interlude played over the studio speakers.

"We're off the air," Henry's voice announced over the intercom. "Thomas, are you all right?"

I realized I had been gazing into nothingness ever since I announced the commercial break. I forced myself back to reality. Wendy was staring.

I cursed. "Yeah, Henry, I'm fine."

Wendy let out a derisive breath and raised her eyebrows. "This job really is getting to you, isn't it?"

"You don't understand, do you, Wendy? It isn't the job that's getting to me, it's—it's this. As if the planet weren't in a big enough mess as it is, now we find out that in three days we are going to be struck by the biggest rock anyone has ever seen. Is that not enough reason to be upset?"

"Thomas, the silly thing is going to land in the Atlantic, for crying out loud. We'll just have to make sure all the boats and things are out of the way. It's not like it's going to ruin our lives or anything."

I marvelled at how difficult it is for a small mind to house a large concept like global ecological disaster. "Oh, really? What about all the ocean life that will be killed? This meteor could knock a hole in the food chain big enough to drive a delivery truck through. And what about the shock wave? How about a tidal wave crashing over the British Isles— wouldn't that be nice?" I knew I was red-faced and raging, but I did not care. Wendy was stupid and I needed to vent.

"Oh, settle down, Thomas. You'll give yourself a heart attack."

I directed my next words to the air. "Henry, have Ron contact me as soon as he finishes crunching those numbers. And I want a computer simulation in time for the rebroadcast show."

"You got it, Archbishop."

Wendy would lead off the next segment, so I had some time to collect my thoughts before the camera was on me again. I rearranged the pages of the script and listened with mild disinterest to the Eurobank ad playing on the monitors.

Coming soon—the new subdermal debit cards. Greatest thing since the planet went cashless. No need to carry a bulky card any more— this one gets implanted under your skin.

I glanced up at the monitor, which pictured the palm of someone's hand.

49

The operation is painless.

Right. That is what my dentist always says.

The scar is barely noticeable.

I did notice the distinctive triple-ringlet scar on the hand in the monitor. I glanced down at my own hands. Not for me, thank you. It may be vanity on my part, but I will stick with my current debit card for now. Let the people who keep losing their cards go subdermal.

As the commercial ended, Kaitlin Murray counted down the final seconds and pointed at Wendy, who smiled for the camera before beginning. "Welcome back to 'Global News Tonight.' Joshua ben-David returned to Jerusalem today from the World Cabinet summit in Rome."

In the video clip that appeared in the monitors to be hovering over Wendy's right shoulder, thousands of Israelis pressed against police barricades in an effort to get closer to the dark, slender man emerging from a black limousine. He smiled and waved to the crowd. The people waved more excitedly and some began to hop up and down. Several children close to the barricade waved palm branches at King ben-David as he strode along the guarded aisle that led to the Temple Mount.

"The Israelis were more than happy to see their king on the second anniversary of the completion of the new Temple and the reinstitution of ancient Hebrew forms of worship. King Joshua, you will remember, resolved the Arab-Israeli conflict and sponsored the rebuilding of the Temple. It is apparent that the nation of Israel holds a special place in the heart of the world's most powerful leader, since he reportedly left Rome early to attend the celebration in Jerusalem."

Several priests in Levitical robes guarded a lamb near a huge altar that smoked with sacrificial fire. King Joshua took the lamb from the priests and carried it up the steps of the altar, where the High Priest stood bedecked in finer robes than the other priests. Except for the king's tailored suit, the scene looked as though it could have been lifted directly from the pages of the Old Testament. The video clip ended as the king handed the lamb to the High Priest. But I knew what happened next.

I stopped at my desk to see if Ron Sadler had finished his calculations. There was nothing on the computer from him, so I decided to continue my research on the Israeli miracle workers.

The miracle men were indeed all Israelis, but all were from different families. Not one of them seemed to have any connection to any other one. In fact, they seemed not to have anything in common with each other except for a shared ethnic background and the fact that they all started appearing in news reports about the time of the Great Disappearance, three and a half years ago.

Then there was something.

I almost missed it, but a Jordanian reporter in Amman three years ago filed a report that was cross-indexed under "Jewish cults." I downloaded the full report into my computer and read it. The reporter did not know where these men came from, but he suspected they were Essenes. I rubbed my chin thoughtfully. <u>Very interesting</u>. I knew of this particular cult from some research I had done years ago for a feature broadcast on the Middle East. I had not used the information for the broadcast—it simply lay in the back of my mind amidst all the other seldom-used bits of trivia one picks up with continued research and reporting. I suppose you could call it an occupational hazard.

A dark shadow fell on the desk, and I turned to see the backlit silhouette of a broad-shouldered man with short, fuzzy hair. I could not make out the features of the man's face, but I recognized my friend instantly. "Hello, Henry."

Straight white teeth blazed in a Cheshire Cat grin. "Always working, huh, Thomas? Come on, let's go get a bite."

"Oh, thanks, but I am waiting for Dr. Sadler's data."

"Ron says it'll be a while. Besides, I'm buying."

An audible growl emanated from my abdomen. It was seven-thirty and I had not eaten all day. I stood and said, "It sounds as though I have been out-voted."

Henry's idea of fine dining was Mort's Diner just two blocks from the station. The food, while certainly not gourmet fare, was at least edible. It was the atmosphere I hated. Situated on the corner of an old building, the diner's front two walls were iron-barred windows. The back walls were a dirty cream color from years of cigarette-smoking patrons and the occasional kitchen fire. I picked one of the few booths with undamaged seat vinyl and plopped down. Henry eased himself into the seat opposite and eyed me critically as I wiped imaginary debris from the table.

Henry chuckled, deepening the subtle crow's feet by his eyes. "Thomas, you're incorrigible," he said. "There's nothing wrong with this place. I've eaten here for years, and so have you, my friend." With that last phrase, Henry jabbed my chest with his big, beefy forefinger, yanking me back to reality.

"I'm sorry, Henry, I was just thinking."

"What about?"

"Dirt."

"Now, don't start in on the diner. You know what a special place it has in my heart."

I allowed myself a weak smile. "No, not that kind of dirt. Dirt in the air. Meteorite dust. If Sadler is right in his initial findings, and I hope he's wrong, Mother Earth could be in for a rough ride."

A haggard-looking waitress sauntered up to the table and asked us for our order. I ordered a BLT with a sour dill pickle on the side and iced tea, and Henry said he would have the double cheeseburger with fries and a beer.

After the waitress left, Henry returned to the unfinished conversation. "You don't really think this meteorite thing is a big deal, do you? I mean, I know you have a flair for the dramatic, but Wendy's right—this thing's going to land in the ocean, far away from any civilization. There might be a tidal wave, but that should be it."

"I don't know. We'll just have to see how the numbers crunch, but if this thing is big enough, it could throw tons of debris into the air and create a cataclysmic greenhouse effect."

"Just great," Henry exclaimed, throwing his arms into the air in a gesture of mock exasperation. "Now the global warming folks will really have something to talk about."

I ignored Henry's attempt at levity. "Scientists' best guess is that some sort of global disaster killed off the dinosaurs. I just hope we're not next in line."

Henry paused for the briefest of moments, his normally bright eyes suddenly staring into empty space. Quickly shaking out of it, he sat up straight and spoke in a deep, resounding baritone. "Enough of that. Thomas Beckett, Archbishop of Canterbury, I, Henry the Second, King of Great Britain, hereby order you to cheer up."

I recognized my cue and dipped my head deferentially. "Of course, my prince. Forgive me. I was terribly remiss in my duties. I should be keeping you entertained."

Henry relaxed and smiled. "That's better. Say, what have you found out about your glow-worm preacher?"

Good. A change in subject. I leaned over the table and said, "I think he's an Essene."

Henry leaned over, too, until our faces were mere inches apart and whispered, "What's an Essene?"

52

"Ancient Hebrew religious sect. Males only, very austere living conditions, and very zealous. Sort of a cross between a Benedictine monk and a Shiite Muslim."

Henry raised his eyebrows and sat back in the bench seat. "Monks with an attitude. I like it."

"That's not all. Their main purpose, their raison d'etre, is to create a holy society for the coming of the Messiah. The Essenes are the only reason we have many ancient manuscripts."

"Why have I never heard of these guys?"

"Have you heard of the Dead Sea Scrolls?"

"Sure. Everybody has."

"Then you have heard of the Essenes."

"Interesting," Henry said, crossing his arms. "So where do these Essenes live? Where do they come from?"

"Well, that's the problem. The best information I can gather is that the organization has been dead for centuries. But these miracle workers fit the bill, so . . ."

"So maybe everybody is wrong. Hey, stranger things have happened."

The waitress brought the food to the table, and we nodded our thanks. I picked up my BLT and took a savage bite. Even though my stomach had been growling like a caged lion since Henry had mentioned getting something to eat, I had not felt hungry until I smelled the food.

Henry paused long enough to savor the aroma of his cheeseburger and fries before speaking again. "Speaking of this Essene, or whatever he is, I heard your conversation with Linda this morning."

I stopped chewing and waited for Henry to continue.

"Listen, Thomas, I—I don't know what's wrong with Linda. She's been acting really weird lately. I'm having a tough time just keeping her off my black behind, so I can't offer you any support for the way she treated you. But I do want you to know that I'm behind you on this story. You need anything, just let me know."

I put my sandwich down and picked up a napkin. "I appreciate that, Henry. How do you propose we air the story without Her Highness's approval?"

"Ah," Henry said around a mouthful of cheeseburger. "That's where my profound knowledge and expertise come into play."

"Really."

"Yep. 'Cause I happen to know that Ms. Friedman is going on vacation next week. Yours Truly will be Global News God, and we can run stories about fat people eating their way out of chocolate factories if we want to."

A slow smile stole across my face as I raised the glass of iced tea to my lips.

"You just be ready with that story when I say go," Henry said.

"I will," I said and dove into my sandwich with reckless abandon.

Upon returning to my desk, I was greeted again by the e-mail icon. Henry followed me into the cubicle and sat on the desk while I pulled the message up.

"It's from Sadler. He says the computer simulation is ready, and . . . Oh, no."

"What?"

"It's worse than I thought. Black Knight is going to . . ."

Henry got up from his perch on the desk and bent over slightly to read the message. "Total mass, blah, blah, force of impact, yeah, yeah—whoa. A thirty-three percent reduction in visible light reaching the earth's surface, but a five percent increase in the amount of heat retained by the atmosphere? Better cancel that vacation to Fort Lauderdale. No suntan for me this year."

I looked up at Henry. "How can you be so glib? Don't you understand? A five percent increase in the heat we get from the sun means ecological mayhem. True global warming. There will be mass flooding as the polar ice caps melt."

Henry was immediately serious. He knew as well as I the implications of that kind of flooding. Every nuclear power plant in the world by design had to be put near a large body of water. With nuclear power plants flooded out, we would have a global energy crisis.

"And food shortages as crops fail," I continued, "and with famine comes widespread disease and a host of other things we're not prepared for. We humans think we're so bloody invincible, and along comes this glorified rock that threatens to destroy us all."

Henry took in a shaky breath and patted my shoulder. "Nobody promised you fair, Old Buddy. Anyway, I'm sure we'll get out of this scrape. Most people are pretty clever when it comes to survival, and the ones who aren't . . . well, they won't be around for very long. Maybe this will be good, in the end, you know."

"Survival of the fittest?" I said, unable to restrain the bitter edge.

"Yeah, something like that. I know it sounds cruel; it's not politically correct or anything, but . . ." Henry's eyes wandered back to the computer screen as his voice caught in his throat and a muscle in his jaw twitched twice. He stared at the screen for a long moment before turning and walking wordlessly away.

I tried to envision the next five years, or even the next five months. The initial impact would be similar to a nuclear explosion at sea level, but this would be larger by several orders of magnitude than any nuclear explosion earth had ever seen. After the airborne shockwave, a tidal wave of proportions Ron would only speculate about would emanate from ground zero. Millions of gallons of water would vaporize along with the meteorite itself. There would be enough debris to encircle the earth with a cloud fifty feet thick. A shiver ran down my spine as I tried to find the silver lining in this large, dark cloud.

Well, at least we now have a global government in place. Joshua ben-David and the World Cabinet are probably better equipped to organize the earth's resources during a time like this than any ruling body we've ever had before.

Linda Friedman's voice startled me. "Thomas. Henry. In my office, now."

I launched out of my chair and fell into step with Henry, who had just emerged from the men's room. I shot Henry a quizzical look, but the director refused to meet my gaze. Henry's jaw muscle still twitched once every few seconds.

Once all of us were in Linda's office, she stood behind her desk and said, "Close the door." I shut the door. Linda picked up an envelope from her desk and handed it to Henry. "You two are going to Israel," she said.

"Israel?" Henry said, looking into the envelope. "What's up?"

"A very big mess. Here's the scoop: the Tel Aviv branch called just now. We've got two men in Jerusalem giving King ben-David all kinds of trouble."

"So?" Henry shrugged. "Why doesn't the IDF just get rid of them?"

"If you'll shut up for a minute, I'll explain." Linda's face was getting red. Henry raised his eyebrows at her outburst. Linda continued, "Apparently, no one can touch these people. So far, fifteen soldiers have died trying."

"What do you mean, they died trying?"

"Something wrong with your ears, Beckett? They died, as in 'no longer living.' Don't ask me how. They just dropped dead."

"You can't tell us anything?"

55

"The soldiers tried to arrest the two men, and when they did, one of the men pointed at them and yelled something, and they dropped dead. Just like that. And if I knew any more than that, I wouldn't have to send you two heroes overseas to report the story, now would I?"

"What about the reporters at the Tel Aviv branch?" Henry asked. "Why aren't they taking this story?"

Linda turned abruptly and walked to the window. She stared into the inky night for several heartbeats before answering. "They're scared. Six seasoned reporters and an entire staff of dimwits are scared right out of their pants. It's incredible. I couldn't pay any one of them enough to go to Jerusalem right now. But that's irrelevant, since most of them no longer work for GNN." She turned slowly to face me. "You're not frightened, are you?"

"Of course not."

"Good. You've been acting strangely the last few days. Just making sure." Linda's tone was conciliatory, but her facial expression was vaguely threatening.

My thoughts went back to my last conversation with Linda. <u>She knows that this story is somehow linked to my story on the Essene preacher, and she hates having to send me to cover it. Is that why Henry's going along? To make sure I remain unbiased?</u>

Linda said, "You two better get moving. Your plane leaves in an hour."

Chapter 10: Joshua

The morning sun had already heated the tarmac at the Ben-Gurion airport in Tel Aviv to the point that the tower appeared wavy and distorted in the distance. I whispered a curse. I hated the desert.

The tires of the big airliner screeched in protest as they made contact with the hot pavement, and the jet engines roared briefly, slowing the plane to taxi speed. Henry sat across the aisle, staring out the opposite window and mirroring my glum mood.

"Welcome to Israel," Henry said. Then his phone rang, and he pulled it out of his back pocket. "Wilson here. Good. We're on the runway now. Be there in five." Henry snapped the phone shut and said, "Limo's here. They'll meet us at the gate."

I nodded and looked out the window again. "It's been a long time, Henry."

"You haven't been here since the war, have you?"

"No," I said, then shuddered. "What a mess that was."

As soon as Henry and I settled into the back seat of the limo, the driver floored the accelerator, causing the tires to screech briefly in protest.

"Are we in a hurry?" I said to the driver.

"My instructions are to get you gentlemen to Jerusalem as quickly as possible."

Henry chuckled. "Sit back and enjoy the ride, Thomas."

The ride to Jerusalem was fast and rough. We would have preferred a short helicopter flight, but King Joshua ben-David's treaty with Israel included a provision that gave the Israeli Defense Forces sole control of the airspace over all the land won in Ezekiel's War. This land included all of Israel as well as Jordan, Syria, Lebanon, and Egypt to the border of the Red Sea. Except for the flights in and out of the major airports at Tel Aviv and Amman, the IDF generally prohibited commercial and private aircraft from invading their now-expansive domain.

Through the patronage of the world's most powerful leader, the tiny, constantly besieged nation of Israel was finally at peace and enjoying the greatest period of prosperity she had known in over two thousand years.

When we reached the Old City, Henry and I pushed through the crowd in our usual ways. I ducked in and through openings like a running back determined to reach the end zone, and Henry played the part of a defensive lineman, shoving all obstacles out of the way of his hulking progress. Our individual methods had served us well over the years, with Henry earning more return shoves and curses than I had. Fortunately for Henry, few people, after getting a good look at him, seemed motivated to do more than that.

Making my way to the police line through the close-knit crowd that swayed like ocean swells, I did not notice the palace. But when I was stopped by a soldier, what I saw took my breath away.

Joshua ben-David's builders had to have cleared out several blocks of Israeli residences just to lay the foundation. Rising ten stories in the air, the roof of the structure was supported by pillars that were almost Roman in appearance, ornately decorated with an extravagance reminiscent of Baroque cathedrals, minus the human sculptures. The gold-trimmed roof line was a cross between a Muslim mosque and a Japanese pagoda. Every one of the too-numerous windows was framed in gold, and the glass entryway was at least fifty feet high. The building sat twenty-five yards behind a high metal fence that was probably electrified and most definitely well guarded. Clearly, Joshua ben-David was a man who loved opulent living. And security.

I asked a stout middle-aged man standing next to me what was happening. I was not sure if the surprise that registered on the man's round face was because I had spoken Hebrew, or because he thought that only a boob could possibly not know what had caused such a stir. I smiled and explained that I was a reporter, and that seemed to satisfy him.

He scratched his chin, and his thick black beard swallowed his fingers up to the second knuckle. "The two blasphemers just left," he said, nodding to indicate their direction. "We are waiting to hear what King ben-David has planned for those false prophets."

I stood on my toes and tried to see where the two men might have gone.

The Israeli tugged on my sleeve. "You won't see them," he said. "They are like the wind. They come and go as they please, and no one stops them." He raised his eyebrows when I told him of my intention to interview them. He said, "Has a man ever caught the wind?"

The big glass front doors opened, and a medium-built man in a dark suit stepped out, followed by four body guards. As he walked toward the gate, his steps seemed a little unsteady. I had only met Joshua Cohen once before, on the day I interviewed him following Ezekiel's War. Even though he stands less than an inch taller than I, King ben-David is an imposing figure. His youthful, chiseled features hide a keener intellect than any I've ever encountered. He is the shrewdest diplomat I know, as evidenced by the peace he has almost singlehandedly brought to the war-torn Middle East. Joshua ben-David is a man who knows what he wants and exactly how to get it.

The crowd cheered—we all did—at the approach of King ben-David, ruler of a third of the planet and the most powerful man on earth. Our cheers gradually died down as the king stood in the open gate and held up his hands for silence. King Joshua lowered his arms, and an almost supernatural hush fell on us, as if our lives depended on what this man would say.

He paused. I noticed that his normally dark face looked ashen, as if he had just been frightened.

When he spoke, I jumped. Then I realized he was wearing a hidden microphone that transmitted to a concealed sound system somewhere, though I could not tell even where the loudspeakers were. The overall effect, even demystified, was quite astounding.

This god-like voice that resounded and reverberated in the streets and soared over the crowd noise seemingly emanated from a man who stood only five feet nine inches tall. "Children of Israel," he began in perfect Oxford English, "and children of earth. You are all curious, as you should be, about the two men who left this place moments ago. You are perhaps a little disturbed that they were able to overcome my security measures and walk directly into the royal palace. Some of you, I believe, are even angry at the arrogant presumption of these men to accost your king so." He smiled. "I share your sentiments."

A light chuckle swept through the crowd, and the tension I had felt seconds ago vanished like a cloud of steam in the kitchen.

The king paused before continuing. "You may all rest assured, however, that at no time were we in any danger. We granted the men a brief audience, during which time they expressed their displeasure at our rule, much as you saw them do yesterday in the Court of Israel. Only this time, no one died. They are a strong force, these enemies of Israel, these enemies of the truth. But they will not succeed. For I, Messiah ben-David, will be their peace, even as I have brought peace to the children of Abraham."

At this, a shout ensued that was so loud I had to cover my ears. I turned around and saw even more people in the crowd than before. Where had they all come from? Then, from somewhere on my left, a chant started and spread like the wave at a football game: "<u>Hosanna!</u> <u>Moshaich!</u>"

These secular Israelis, most of whom had a religious nature equal to the gang lords in the American Midwest, now shouted praises to their long-awaited Messiah. His face having regained its color, the man who used to be Joshua Cohen, European diplomat, basked in the glow of his native nation's adoration.

It may have been my imagination—to this day I am still unsure— but at that moment, it seemed that King Joshua ben-David was physically transformed. He became bigger than life, and I was struck with the sudden, irrational impression that he was invincible. For a few brief moments, I forgot about the disaster promised by the Black Knight. I was filled with an unexplainable sense of security in the presence of King Joshua. As long as he reigned, there were no insurmountable odds, no solutions he could not give us. No mere meteorite could destroy us.

I was surprised at my thoughts. They were certainly not the objective analysis of a seasoned reporter. I was beginning to think more like a religious devotee. Why? Was it his charisma? I doubt it. I am far too skeptical to be taken in by a dynamic personality or the trappings of success. Looking back on it now, I believe all of us in that crowd were under the influence of some outside force.

At the time, though, I did not care. All that mattered was the man, the Son of David. And all any of us knew was that as long as he lived, there would be peace and prosperity first for the nation of Israel, then for the world.

Chapter 11: High Priest

After several unsuccessful attempts at tracking down the mystery men, we turned our attention inward. King ben-David's schedule would not allow for an interview, but Henry managed to arrange for me to talk with the Hebrew High Priest.

Ezra ben-Hadad is the stereotypical ultra-orthodox Jew. A Hebrew's Hebrew. I am certain that even his toilet habits are governed by Levitical Law. Since Henry and I, Gentiles that we are, could not meet in his "office," an anteroom of the new Temple, Rabbi ben-Hadad was gracious enough to come to our hotel suite.

He came to the door dressed in black from neck to toe. His jet black beard and side curls showed fewer streaks of gray than I would have expected from a man in his late fifties, and they dropped below the collar of his shirt, giving the visual effect of a hood and mask. Only his dark hands, narrow nose, and dark brown eyes were visible. Two IDF security guards in plain clothes followed him in, and a third stayed out in the hall. Another almost certainly waited in the limousine outside in case a fast getaway was necessary. I consider precautions like these healthy paranoia. Evidently, so do the IDF.

He smiled warmly. "Good afternoon, Mr. Beckett." His accent was light and lilting, like that of many highly educated Israelites.

One of the IDF guards waved an electronic device around in the air to detect explosives while the other walked around the room checking the security of the windows.

Forcing myself to ignore their ministrations, I returned the High Priest's smile and shook his outstretched hand. "Good afternoon, Rabbi. Thank you so much for agreeing to this interview." Over my shoulder I could hear Henry arguing with one of the guards over his recording equipment. Evidently, all was not <u>kosher</u>.

"Of course it has a laser in it," Henry said. "That's what it uses to record the sound—it's not going to hurt anybody." He turned to me with his palms open, pleading. "Thomas, you know these people better than I do—can you talk some sense into this technophobe?"

I was about to open my mouth when Rabbi ben-Hadad barked an order in Hebrew, and the guard backed away.

"Forgive my assistant," the Rabbi said. "It is his job, you understand."

"Yes, of course," I said. "Now, if you would like to get

comfortable on the couch over there, we can begin the interview."

"Rabbi, you are recognized by many as a world spiritual leader of equal standing with the Pope. You may actually be more popular than the Pontiff among the global community. But five years ago, it was not this way. How do you account for that?"

"It is simple, Mr. Beckett. Our Temple has been rebuilt. The God of Abraham, Isaac, and Jacob has restored the fortunes of His chosen people, and I have been chosen from among the sons of Levi to be the leader of the regathered tribes of Israel, together with King Joshua ben-David."

I leaned forward in my chair. This was the opening I had hoped for. "Rabbi, many Israelis refer to the King as if he were the promised Messiah. Today, he even referred to himself using that title. Do you believe that King ben-David is the Messiah your people have waited for all these centuries?"

"Absolutely I believe this." The High Priest's eyes shone with smoldering intensity. He most certainly did believe what he was saying. Every word of it. Then he added, "Absolutely. There is no doubt."

"Really? Why Joshua Cohen—"

"ben-David," he corrected, chiding me with a wagging index finger.

"Yes, of course, ben-David. But why him and not someone else?"

"Let me ask you something, Mr. Beckett. When you were a child, how did you know that the man living in your house was your father?"

He had blind-sided me. Momentarily stunned, I stammered, "Well, I guess because, well—"

I caught a glimpse of Henry in my peripheral vision. He had the camera pointed at me. Figures. He always loved to catch the unflappable Thomas Beckett on camera during those rare moments when something had me flapped. I focussed my attention back on my job.

"Because he fulfilled the role of the father, yes?" the Rabbi said. "You knew him not by his appearance or his words, but by the part he played in your life, did you not? So it is with us, Mr. Beckett. "Since our Temple was destroyed in the first century of the Common Era, we as a people have longed to see it rebuilt and to have a homeland again. Joshua ben-David has helped us rebuild the Temple. He has ensured the security of our nation. We in Israel know him as Messiah because he has played out the role of Messiah for us."

"Rabbi," I said, "Messiah is a title few people in our North American audience understand. Could you explain?"

He smiled. "Yes, of course. The Law and the Prophets tell us of a king that God will raise up out of the lineage of David, a king who will 'rule the nations with a rod of iron' and who will reign forever."

I played Everyman and acted surprised. "Well, Rabbi, that is certainly a tall order, even for King ben-David. Anyone can see that he certainly rules the nations, but what about living forever? How is the King going to accomplish that?"

The Rabbi leaned back on the couch as the first hint of a wry smile curled one side of his mouth beneath his thick black beard. "At this moment, only King ben-David and I know how this will happen. But soon, the glory of Messiah will be revealed to the world. He now rules one third of the earth. Soon, all nations will follow him."

"Can you give us a hint?"

"You Americans have no patience," he said, dismissing my comment with a wave of his hand. "Israel has waited thousands of years to see prophecy fulfilled. I think you can wait a short while longer to see the conclusion of this matter."

"We'll be looking forward to it. I just have one more question, Rabbi. You said that King ben-David has played out the role of Messiah, and that is how you recognize him as Messiah. But others throughout history have played out various aspects of what the Law and the Prophets have to say about the Messiah—Jesus of Nazareth comes to mind. . . ." I knew from the darkening of his face I had committed a grievous offense.

He leaned forward and our eyes locked. His voice was low and menacing. "Don't talk to me about the Nazarene, Mr. Beckett. That man and his tiny following were impostors from the start." He pointed a finger at me. It quivered with rage. "He was no Messiah. He ruled <u>nothing</u>. He was a crazy man, like your David Koresh a decade ago."

Should I back off or press in? I decided to press in. "Rabbi, you and the Pope have met on several occasions for the purpose of fostering unity between the world's two greatest religions. Will Christians find your words offensive?"

He sat back up and the fire in his eyes abated. My attack was successful. "Mr. Beckett, I have no desire to tell anyone what religion to have, or even to have any. God has revealed Himself to the nation of Israel in very special ways—the ways revealed to us through the Torah and the Prophets. I realize, however, that He reveals Himself to others differently. The Pope himself has done much in recent months to bring together all the world's religions. God does not give us the luxury of an easy interpretation. As the Pope likes to say, 'The Divine is the eternally manifesting Energy in which everything is mysteriously arising.' So you see, Mr. Beckett, the world is large enough to contain all interpretations of God, even atheistic and agnostic ones. We can all learn to live together. I am sure Christians will forgive my little outburst, since the Hebrew religion is my area of expertise, and our God is a jealous God."

I managed a wan smile. "Yes, I am sure they will forgive you." I then asked Rabbi ben-Hadad about King Joshua's plans to deal with Black Knight. He assured me that preparations were being made. Coastal cities that bordered the Atlantic were being evacuated, the World Health Organization, along with other disaster relief groups, was stocking up on supplies, and the world's finest ecologists and agricultural scientists were formulating plans to deal with the long-term effects of the meteorite's impact.

The High Priest painted a picture that was far rosier than I thought possible, but it all centered around Joshua ben-David's ability to organize earth's people and resources in order to deal with this crisis. Knowing that King Joshua was personally coordinating the plans and the planners bolstered my confidence, but the High Priest's nearly evangelistic support of ben-David lessened my respect for the man sitting on the couch before me. I knew this was an irrational reaction, since Rabbi ben-Hadad was merely expressing the same confidence in Joshua ben-David that was felt by all who spent any time listening to him. I felt the same way about the king that the Rabbi did, but for some reason, I thought less of him for expressing it.

I felt an odd sense of relief when the High Priest and his entourage left.

Henry gazed out the window as the limo pulled away from the curb. He said, "There go all the King's men."

"You can say that again. Was that the High Priest or the President of the Joshua Cohen fan club?" I plopped down on the couch.

Henry shook a finger at me.

"Yes, I know—ben-David. But who is he, really?"

Henry loosened his tie and took the camera off its tripod. "We're not gonna find out from anyone around here. Wonder if we could track down his parents."

"No," I said. "They died twenty years ago."

"Friends?"

"People like Joshua ben-David don't have friends. They have staff members."

"No, you white-bred pretty boy, I mean his old friends. The boys from the 'hood."

I snorted. "Good luck. I've been researching this guy for the better part of three years now and haven't found one yet. It's almost as if Joshua Cohen and all that he was died the day King ben-David was crowned." I got up and walked to the window. "Maybe before. . .I don't know."

Chapter 12: Prophets of Fire

The call came about ten minutes after the High Priest had left.

I had stepped out to get a couple of sodas when the phone rang and Henry answered it. I returned to the room in time to hear the terse end of the conversation.

"We'll be there in five minutes," Henry said and slammed the phone shut.

"What is it?"

"The wackos—they're back."

I gave Henry his soda, and we rushed out the door.

No matter how hard he tries, one man can never be heard over a shouting, belligerent crowd. However, these two men somehow managed.

They were each almost as tall as Henry. The one with the stocky frame did most of the talking, while the wiry one looked around and added comments here and there. Their sun-darkened skin shone with a glow that might have been olive oil, or it might have been the same bizarre luminescence I had encountered just a couple of days before. Since it was impossible to tell for certain in the brightness of the Israeli noon hour, I comforted myself with the assumption they had been anointed with oil.

As an American, I find the Middle Eastern custom of dousing someone with oil as a sign of honor and authority strange at best. But as they moved around, braving the angry mob and plying the crowd with their words, I was struck with the thought that the faces of powerful and brave people ought to shine.

Their message was basically the same one I had heard from the mouth of the Hebrew standing in New York on the wreck of a police car. Repent, the time is at hand, etc. I scanned the crowd, trying to detect anyone wearing a trench coat or something else big enough to hide a weapon. But this was Jerusalem, where firearms are as common as remote controls. The search was useless. I could only hope that no one would shoot these two before I had a chance to interview them.

The stocky one preached while the thin man stomped around in a frenetic perimeter near the crowd. "Hear me, all of you!" he shouted. "We have told you the end is near, that Messiah Yeshua is returning soon. If you will not believe this, at least believe what the prophet Daniel has stated. When you see the abomination of desolation, run to the mountains! Seek refuge! Save your lives, because from that day forward, the true nature of the false Messiah will be revealed. Only then can Messiah Yeshua come back from Heaven to establish His kingdom."

Somewhere in the mass of humanity a woman yelled, "King ben-David is our Messiah!"

The pacing prophet spotted the woman, pointed at her and shouted, "Silence! Shalom."

The woman opened her mouth, thought better of it, and did her best to shrink into the group of people around her. The crowd as a whole became more quiescent.

Satisfied with his audience's behavior, the speaker continued, "We have also told you, and proven with signs from Heaven, that the man called Joshua ben-David is no Messiah, but an imposter who serves the Accuser of Mankind. We give you now the same message we gave to him earlier today. The Blessed One has numbered the king's days. That blasphemer is going to eternal torment, with his master, Satan. The prophet Daniel speaks of this king when he says, "And he shall confirm the covenant with many for one week. And in the midst of the week he shall cause the sacrifice and the oblation to cease . . .""

The next thing was a blur.

A short man in Levitical robes screamed a curse and dove from the edge of the crowd, arms flailing the air. But his target stood still.

The thin man went into action. He strode toward the man, pointed, and said in a voice that was as loud as ben-David's amplified speech, "Touch not God's anointed."

If I never believed in miracles before, I did at that moment.

With his next step not yet complete, the charging priest burst into flames. His body skidded to a clumsy stop at the feet of the preacher. For the span of a heartbeat, the crowd became deathly silent. The only sounds were the crackle and hiss of burning flesh. The preacher placidly stood his ground, like a blind man before a mime. There was extreme sadness etched on his face.

There was no scream, only a look of shock on the horrified, charred, almost featureless face. It had all happened so quickly, I doubted the man had felt anything.

The crowd did not so much gasp as it did groan. They had seen this happen before. The groan was sympathy for the poor fool who threw himself at an unbeatable foe, a lifeguard fighting a tidal wave.

"Did you—" I looked at Henry. He nodded dumbly, holding the camera steady on the burning corpse.

The thin man took over as if nothing had happened. These men were cold-blooded and heartless. Or they were men with a mission.

"Children of Israel, how long will you fight against the God of Abraham, Isaac, and Jacob? Your hearts are hard." Our hearts are hard? You're the one who just got away with murder. "Just as in the days of Moses, when Pharaoh hardened his heart, so it is today. Judgments have been decreed, and desolations to the end, just as the prophets foretold. You will see with your eyes the wrath of Heaven poured out on a disobedient and rebellious people—first Israel, then the nations."

The thin man paused, and an air of anticipation swelled and crackled like electricity. The stocky preacher held his hands at shoulder level, palms up, eyes closed, mouth moving silently.

The thin man continued, "The word of the Lord came to me, saying, 'Tell my people Israel, and tell the nations, this is what the Lord God says: I searched the world for a pure heart and found it lacking. You have rejected the life I offered in my Son Yeshua of Nazareth, taking an imposter in His stead." Yeshua of Nazareth? The High Priest isn't going to like that, I thought, remembering his fierce reaction to that name during my interview with him. "'Therefore, since you have rejected the light that I offer, a mountain will be cast into the sea, and your skies will be darkened, and the sun and the moon will grow dim. Now look for Me as intently as you look for the light of day, and you will live.' Thus says the Lord."

Without another word, the two men picked a direction and walked through the crowd that parted like the Red Sea in that old Charlton Heston film.

I ran across the open circle toward the swath they had cut while Henry backtracked through the crowd. The preachers were fast. They had cleared the outer fringes of the crowd before I caught up with them, and Henry came huffing along.

"Excuse me," I said. No response. I closed the gap between us. "Hey! Stop."

The two men stopped and turned to face Henry and me. "What do you want with us, American?" the thin man said.

I held my hands up in a gesture of supplication. "I just want to talk to you."

They looked at each other as if conferring. They said nothing. But they communicated something, because when they regarded me again, the thin man said, "Walk with us."

We walked in silence, neither one of them answering my questions, until we were completely out of the city.

"Who are you?" I said, staring at the two men. I dared not touch them.

"Turn the recording equipment off."

I nodded at Henry and he complied.

"Who we are is not as important as the message we bring," said the stocky one.

"We have to call you something. 'The Miracle Men' sounds too Hollywood for my tastes." A pause. "All right, then, what do other people call you?"

Another silent conference transpired, and then they did something that seemed at the time more miraculous than the priest bursting into flames. Together, they smiled. "Men call us the 'Sons of Thunder'."

<u>Why does that sound familiar? Something very old. . . something from my childhood?</u> "Hm. Very dramatic, I'm sure, but I have an audience of over 200 million people worldwide. They are going to want to know your names."

"Very well," the thin one said. "My name is James—"

"—and I am John," the stocky one concluded.

"James and John." <u>James and John. Sons of Thunder. That's it. Two of the disciples of Jesus of Nazareth.</u> "Is your father's name Zebedee?" I said, failing to hide the chuckle in my voice.

"No," said John, suddenly serious again. "And if it were, that would be even less important to our mission than our own names."

"It's obvious you're on a mission. Please tell me about it."

"Our mission is to proclaim the truth of the Living God and to testify of Messiah Yeshua, our Righteous King and Judge of the Earth."

"Who gave you this mission?"

James said, "If you saw what happened today, you need not ask that question."

He was right, of course, but the reporter in me wanted some juicy quote I could relate to our viewing audience. A raving religious nut was always good for business, but these men were too calm, too cool-headed. "So you claim that Jesus of Nazareth is the true Messiah. That can't be a popular viewpoint here in Jerusalem."

"Let God be true and every man a liar," said James.

"We are no more interested in popularity, Mr. Beckett, than was the prophet Elijah when he called down fire from Heaven."

I had forgotten that Henry was walking with us, and when he spoke, I jumped. "But aren't you afraid of King ben-David? You guys are standing toe-to-toe against the most powerful man in the world."

The two men doubled over with laughter, leaving Henry and me to shrug our shoulders in uncomprehending silence. We waited for the Sons of Thunder's storm of hilarity to pass.

John stood, wiping tears from his eyes. "I am sorry, but you must understand—God laughs at His enemies. We do not fear your king, because we have been sealed by the Holy Spirit of God. Joshua Cohen has no power over us. He can do nothing. You men have seen this with your own eyes, no?"

James said, "We have a mission to tell the world of the number of days allotted to the son of perdition and of the coming of the Son of Man on clouds of glory. Until the time given to us is complete, no one will be able to harm us."

"And on the day we lay down our lives," said John, "know that even then, our lives are hid with God. And He will raise us up on the third day to join Him in glory, so that all the prophet wrote about us will be fulfilled. Until that time, Mr. Beckett, we will overcome the wicked one by the blood of the Lamb and the word of our testimony."

Back in the hotel room, I sipped my Scotch as that last line boomed from John's mouth. The camera cut to me for the final tag.

"There you have it, North America. Strong words spoken against the man many are calling the 'Man of Peace'. What will the king's response be to these violent men? Only time will tell. From Jerusalem, I'm Thomas Beckett."

Henry emerged from the kitchenette with a beer in his hand. He popped the top and sat next to me on the couch. "Thomas, either you have a short memory, or you are the biggest narcissist I know. Didn't you get enough of those two chuckleheads up close and personal today?"

Wendy's face had replaced mine on the screen. She was announcing the commercial break. Red blazer again. Gee, thanks, Wendy.

"Neither," I said, getting up to freshen my drink, "I just like seeing it all come together in a finished product."

"Yeah, I was right. Narcissist."

Chapter 13: The Bullet

First thing that next morning—even before I had taken the first sip of coffee—I checked the latest news stories on the Web. I wanted to find out what preparations were being made to combat the global catastrophe promised by Black Knight.

The meteorite's impact was now less than a day away, and the stories I read were distressing. Worldwide violence went beyond epidemic—it was pandemic. Panic-stricken people raided stores, hoarding food and clothing and anything else they thought they needed to survive the uncertain calamity that Black Knight threatened. I could find nothing from any of the services—CNN, AP, UPI, GNN—that would indicate that any preparations were being made to save resources or lives. Joshua ben-David's promised plan of deliverance had not yet been revealed. I shut the computer off in disgust. <u>How can one man save mankind?</u>

That was when we got word from the royal palace that Joshua ben-David would hold a press conference. There he would announce his plan to save mankind. No one had seen much of the world leader since he had found out about Black Knight. He had holed up with some of the most respected astronomers, ecologists, and physicists in the world in an effort to develop a plan to deal with the threat imposed by the meteorite. Evidently none of that plan had yet made its way beyond the palace walls.

At ten o'clock that morning, we would hear the king's plan.

Henry and I arrived early but still had to fight our way past crowds of the curious as well as several well-armed IDF soldiers.

"For every soldier you recognize," Henry said, "I bet there's at least five in disguise."

He was probably right. Even the security that was visible was tighter than usual. No doubt a product of the paranoia that seemed to be getting to us all. When a large number of people are convinced they are about to die, there is always that small percentage who are suddenly capable of thinking the unthinkable and doing the unspeakable.

The room where the press conference was to be held was in the southwest wing of the king's palace. It was smaller than I had anticipated for such an important event. With seating for no more than four hundred, the room smacked of crowd control.

Richly colored tapestries hung from the ceiling to the floor three stories below along both side walls. My suspicions that the tapestries covered over a multitude of electronic surveillance equipment were confirmed with a quick peek behind one as Henry and I crowded our way toward the front of the room. Feeling the cold hardness of a machine gun barrel between two of my ribs, I decided to move on. IDF soldiers have very little patience with curious reporters.

The front of the room held a large stage that gave the impression that we were at a play rather than a press conference. This setup seemed odd, since I had heard that Joshua ben-David was a serious man, not given to entertainment. Why would he have a theater in his palace?

Henry and I sat down on the outside of the second row, and within minutes a deep, resonant voice boomed over the sound system, "Ladies and gentlemen of the press—King Joshua ben-David."

The stage area lit up as the house lights dimmed by half, drawing everyone's attention to the front of the room, where Joshua stood behind a small lectern.

"Did you—"

"No," Henry said from behind the camera, "it's like he just appeared out of nowhere."

"Neat trick."

"Yeah."

The king began, "Our planet today waits in frightened anticipation for the arrival of the space body called Black Knight. This body will impact the earth somewhere in the Atlantic Ocean later today. Its precise effects are unknown at this time, but one thing is certain—global effects will be felt. I called this press conference to give the world my plan for this time of crisis." He paused and looked at the assembled reporters, his eyes seemingly studying each of us individually. When he finished his perusal, he took a deep breath, and his face seemed to soften a little.

"But first, let me assure each and every inhabitant of planet earth that everything is going to be just fine," he said to the cameras. "There is nothing to fear. Clear your minds for a moment and visualize a peaceful scene as I tell you what is in store for us in the coming days. Are you there in your place of peace? Good. Now I will tell you what we will do about the coming danger.

"Yes, I said <u>we</u>. Now is the time for the children of earth to realize their place in the universe. Our evolution has been progressing more and more rapidly since Mother Earth was cleansed three and a half years ago. But now we must take that final evolutionary leap that will vault us to the heavens where we may truly control our destiny. It will not be easy, but I am here to help you. I am here. I am—"

"Imposter!"

I immediately recognized the prophets' stereophonic voices at the back of the room. "Now, how the—"

"I shoulda known those two would show," Henry grumbled.

The Sons of Thunder strode toward the stage area. "You son of perdition, has the Accuser seduced you so to make you think you can lessen the judgments of the Most High?"

Joshua ben-David, jolted from his peaceful trance, shook with fury, and his normally olive skin turned a shade darker. "Kill these blasphemers!" he screamed, pointing at the two men who showed no sign of slowing their advance. Half a dozen of the uniformed soldiers looked as though they would raise their weapons against the intruders but then thought better of it.

"How is it blasphemy," said James, "to speak the Word of the Lord? You are only a man, yet you have said in your heart, 'I will ascend into heaven, I will exalt my throne above the stars of God: I will sit also upon the mount of the congregation, in the sides of the north . . . I will be like the most High.' But son of dust, I prophesy to you that you are a man and not a god, and though you fall for three days and rise again, you will still meet your end in undying fire."

As James was speaking, John leaped onto the stage and advanced on King Joshua. The king slowly backed away, glaring. John attained the podium and, turning to the cameras, addressed the world.

"This is what the Lord says: 'Though I have spoken, you have not heard; though I cry out, you refuse to listen. You have turned away from the Lord your God, Who created the earth and the heavens, and have chosen instead to follow one who is no god. You have made a god of one no greater than yourselves.

"'But so that you will know that I am the Lord your God and that Yeshua of Nazareth is My Son—you will have no rain on the earth in the day of My wrath. For forty-two months, your crops and your flocks will be without water. Then you will know that I, the Lord, send the rain.

"'Even now, if you repent,' says the Lord, 'I will give you the Living Water that flows from My throne, and you will thirst no longer.'"

Finished with his pronouncement, John stepped to the edge of the stage and hopped to the floor. The room was so quiet I heard his rough robes rustle as he landed on the ground level. The two men walked out of the auditorium unchallenged by soldier or civilian.

Back on the stage, Joshua ben-David struggled to regain his composure. A thick coating of sweat covered his forehead. He approached the podium, and his face hardened into an unreadable death mask.

Henry leaned over and whispered, "How's he gonna handle this?" Raised eyebrows were my silent and sole reply.

"Citizens of earth. What you have just witnessed may have distressed you, but I am glad that it happened, because now you see what we are fighting. Those men, and others like them, would have us revert to the corrupt, narrow way of thinking so prevalent before our planet was cleansed. We must combat their narrow-mindedness by reaching inside, to the god or goddess within to find direction and purpose. My brothers and sisters, I have reached in. I have found the god within, and I am."

"No!"

Heads snapped around. Behind me and to the left. The cry came from a uniformed IDF soldier who could not have been more than nineteen years old.

"My son." Joshua's voice was calm and reassuring. "Do not resist the pull of your inner self. Realize that I am."

The boy now had tears streaming down his face. "No," he yelled. "You are a blasphemer. No man is God. I will never worship you."

The first two or three rounds fired came from that soldier's weapon. Henry and I fell to the floor to avoid the deafening bedlam of gunfire that followed.

When all was silent but for the ringing in our ears, we stood to survey the scene. Joshua ben-David lay on the stage in a pool of blood, a 7.62mm bullet hole in his head.

The boy's body was unrecognizable. My legs began to shake, forcing me to sit down as I considered the implications of what had just happened.

Linda Friedman called less than thirty minutes after I had submitted the story. And when Linda wants to talk to me about a story, it is rarely good news.

"Look, Thomas, I'm very sorry we had to cut your segment down, but it was a decision that had to be made." Her voice was almost patronizing. Even over a bad video phone connection it was obvious she was trying to smooth my ruffled feathers. She never had been good at smoothing anything except that straight brown hair.

"Whose decision, Linda—yours? I know how you feel about this whole story with the Sons of Thunder—"

"You still don't get it, do you, Beckett?" The patronizing tone was gone. "This isn't about some Boy Scout notion you have of journalistic integrity; this is a question of what this story is about. And this story is about the death of the most influential leader this world has seen in ages. It is not about a couple of kooks in bathrobes who walk around stirring up trouble."

"As I recall, Ms. Friedman, the story of those two kooks is what you sent Henry and me over here to cover."

"Maybe so." She faltered. "But the assassination of King ben-David takes precedence."

I had tripped her up. I knew if I controlled my anger, I might be able to get more of my footage approved for the next show. "Have you talked to any of the other producers in town to see what their spin is going to be?"

"Other producers? No, I haven't—"

"There were a lot of reporters in that room today. I'm willing to bet that more than one of them saw a connection between the assassination and the hate speech that preceded it. You wouldn't want AP or Reuters to scoop GNN, would you?"

Linda sighed. "All right, Thomas, you win. We'll air the kook footage. Just remember: you owe me."

"I always have, Linda." I closed the laptop screen and leaned back into the cushions of the couch.

Henry sat in a chair on the opposite wall, grinning. He began clapping. "Thomas Beckett, you are a master."

"Thank you."

"But I really don't understand."

"Understand what?"

"Why you fought so hard to keep those two wackos in your story. A couple of religious bigots. I mean, who cares?"

"Well, it was—" What was it, really? Their relevance to the assassination? No, that was a little questionable. Something one of them said... "Something they said struck me as significant, but now I'm not sure that I remember what it was."

"Let's look at the video again, then."

Henry set up his camera to feed directly into the hotel room TV, and he cued it to the point when the Sons of Thunder made their entrance. We watched until the magic phrase jumped out at me.

"Stop. There," I said. "Back up just a little."

James railed against the king on the screen.

"... you are a man and not a god, and though you fall for three days and rise again, you will still meet your end in undying fire."

"There it is," I said. "Did you hear it?"

"Yeah. Didn't understand a word of it."

I stared at the frozen image of James on the screen and mumbled the words like a chant, "'though you fall for three days and rise again, you will still meet your end in undying fire.' What do you think he's talking about?"

"Thomas, it's just radical, wacko, extremist hate speech, that's all."

"It's more than that, Henry. He's making a prediction. Do you think he is predicting Joshua's assassination?"

Henry laughed. "Yeah, that's good. Predict an assassination that's your fault because you incited religious bigotry in a heavily armed audience. In my book, that ain't no prophecy—that's a game plan."

"Maybe. But what about the part about rising again? Do you think ben-David will recover?"

"Thomas, you were the one who snuck past the guards and went to the man's room. What do you think?"

My heart sank a little as the theory vanished like smoke in a strong wind. The memory of King Joshua lying in an intensive care ward, reduced to a hollow shell that could not even breathe on its own flooded my mind. The conversation between two neurosurgeons as I hid behind a door confirmed the worst. There was too much brain damage. No hope for recovery. The breathing apparatus was merely a formality, a stall for time. The real question now was not if he would recover, but who would replace him as the world's preeminent leader.

Henry had that smug look he always gets when he either knows he's right or he knows he'll win the argument by virtue of his title.

"Okay," I said. "You're right. I'm being ridiculous."

"Thank you. Now you're probably going to bring up all that noise about no rain for—how long was it?"

"Forty-two months."

"Yeah. What's that in people years? Three and a half?"

I nodded.

"That's an awful long drought, Thomas."

I chuckled. "It is rather silly when you think about it in those terms. Still, the debris from Black Knight could cause a sufficient greenhouse effect to prevent rain for an extended period of time."

"Forty-two months, exactly?"

I held up my hands in mock surrender. "All right, Henry, you win. They're wackos."

I slammed the phone down in disgust. Four hours of trying, and still no success getting through to Carolyn and Anthony. I wanted to make sure they were taking proper precautions for the arrival of Black Knight.

However, no one seemed to be sure just what "proper precautions" entailed. People were greeting the impending disaster with a range of emotions from stark terror to blissful anticipation, depending on the significance the event held for them.

In one news report, the priestess Ariel explained that this was no ordinary meteor, but a space ship that housed our alien spirit guides, whose job it was to lead us on in our evolutionary development. She told of a Greenpeace ship that was now en route to the area of the Atlantic where it was felt the space ship would land. Aboard this ship was a complement of some of the finest minds of the scientific community. They had all volunteered to greet our alien friends in a gesture of peace and cooperation.

Another item featured a scraggly-bearded homeless man carrying a sign proclaiming the judgment of God. Wild-eyed and delusional from far too many illegal substances, he continually referred to Black Knight as the "fist of God."

Survivalists in Colorado, Texas, and seven other states were stocking up on food and ammunition. One GNN reporter was fatally shot while approaching a compound in Montana to interview a militia leader.

With the global panic level on the rise, I at least wanted to make sure my son was safe. Anthony might hate the very thought of me, but the feeling was not mutual. For some reason, I felt compelled to let him know that. The front desk clerk had told me two hours ago that the overseas lines had been tied up all day. I kept trying, anyway. But enough was enough.

I lay down on the bed and covered my face with my hands. A toilet flushed, water ran, and Henry emerged from the bathroom.

"Still no Anthony?"

"No. I guess I shouldn't be surprised. Everybody wants to talk to somebody overseas when there is a disaster."

"Yeah," Henry said. "I would suggest a direct satellite linkup, but I've already checked on it."

"Let me guess. The nodes are all tied up."

"Sort of. Most of them have been commandeered by the military—even GNN's corporate linkups. Everything except the dedicated civilian nodes is strictly off limits."

I nodded. "That only makes sense. A dead leader, an uncertain future—I can't believe we staked our planet's destiny on one man." There was a pause as I thought again about the significance of Joshua ben-David's death. "Henry, we may be looking at the beginnings of another war."

"Judging from your track record here in Jerusalem, Thomas, I hope not."

Chapter 14: Impact

A watched pot never boils, but a watched meteorite strikes a thousand times before it ever enters the atmosphere. I leaned forward, studying the television screen as if I could will myself to see the rock that was still thousands of miles above the Atlantic. Thousands of miles, yet mere minutes away.

Henry had grown weary of Wendy's vacuous commentary and muted the sound. Now all that emerged from the set was the image of clear blue sky over an apparently endless sea. The hypnotic blue was unbroken except for the soft, gentle undulation of the waves and a few high wisps of white cloud.

Every few minutes, the perspective would shift slightly as the camera moved. The camera was carried on an unmanned, computer-operated plane that could stay aloft for several days at a stretch. No sense sending a reporter and crew to ground zero of the most cataclysmic natural event in recorded history.

Leave that to Greenpeace. Their ship was circling and had left the range of the aerial camera several minutes ago. It was possible, however unlikely, that they had come to their senses and turned back once they realized that their historic, altruistic mission consisted of allowing themselves to be vaporized by a mountain from space.

Just how much of the impact we would get to see was anybody's guess. My guess was that the drone plane would be destroyed—along with the Greenpeace ship—almost immediately on impact, if not before. Even though the plane was over a mile away from Black Knight's point of impact, the shockwave that would be going ahead of the meteorite would surely be more than enough to crush the tiny aircraft. However, there would still be the photos from the weather satellites.

A small digital clock appeared in the lower left corner of the screen. It resembled the graphics the networks use during timed Olympic events like the Luge, only this clock ran backwards. Less than one minute to impact. The hundredths of seconds blurred by, and even the seconds seemed to quicken their pace to keep up with my pounding heart.

At five seconds remaining, a star moved. At four, it grew brighter, and at three it grew to grotesque proportions. In the final two seconds, the object grew so bright that the camera could no longer compensate, and the screen went white, then static.

The static gave way to a haggard-looking Wendy Matherly and a positively overwrought Ron Sadler sitting behind the GNN news desk. I reached for the remote so I could hear Sadler's evaluation of the impact.

". . .numbers yet on the magnitude of the shock wave, but as soon as they come in, we will report those to you."

Ron and Wendy both paused and looked at a point beyond the cameras. Wendy began speaking before she again locked eyes with the camera. "We are now receiving direct video feed from our GNN affiliate weather satellite. We'll take you to that now . . ."

An image of the earth as seen from high orbit flickered onto the screen. Clouds partly obscured Europe, but France's west coast was clearly visible, as was most of Spain. The image changed, and clouds moved in jerky stages as a tiny white pinprick appeared in the Atlantic several hundred miles to the west of Europe at roughly the same latitude as Portugal. The dot alternately froze and grew until within several seconds it resembled a piece of chalk standing on its end.

"You can begin to see it now," Sadler said. "That white dot in the middle of your screen is the column of steam and debris created by the impact. It's still growing . . ." The chalk tripled in size and began to mushroom. "It looks as though the blast column has reached its greatest height, so I—oh, my." Several of the faint wisps of cloud that had surrounded the growing column of white suddenly parted and wrapped themselves around the expanding mushroom.

As the clouds continued their staccato minuet, Wendy said, "Um, Dr. Sadler, you're obviously disturbed by what you see. Can you tell us what is going on?"

"What? Oh, those clouds . . . are cirrus clouds. I had no idea the blast column would go so high. Oh, this is not good; this is not good at all."

"Can you explain, Doctor?" The image changed again and thin clouds skittered away from the invading blast cloud, piling up on each other in their haste to get away from the relentlessly advancing enemy.

"Explain? Oh, yes, of course. You see, if the debris column travels too high—say, into the stratosphere—then the pollutants it places into the atmosphere will have greater effects than if they were lower. Normally, ashes and dust from a volcanic eruption or meteorite impact will float around for a while in the lower atmosphere until they all come down in the form of some rather dirty rain. But if enough debris is deposited at a high enough altitude, it would not come down as rain at all."

"Then how does it come down, Dr. Sadler?"

"That is precisely the problem, Wendy. It may not come down

for a very long time. We would have a runaway greenhouse effect."

"Greenhouse effect," Henry muttered as another after-shock rumbled through my legs and rattled the window. Outside, I could see the steady advance of the blast debris in the sky. Gone was the cotton white we saw on the satellite film, replaced by an angry gray that roiled and marched across the sky like a sea of locusts. We made eye contact with the cloud early this morning, but the tremors had been going all night.

"So maybe the Sons of Thunder were right, after all."

"What?" Henry glared at me.

"About the drought," I shrugged. "If this greenhouse effect kicks in like Ron thinks it will, then we could be in for some very dry months. Perhaps even forty-two of them, which is longer than anyone had predicted the effects would last."

"Uh-huh. Next thing you'll try to tell me is that you think this whole thing is some kind of judgment from God, or something. Well, I'm not buying."

"No," I said. "I was just noting the coincidence. It's possible these two men have some kind of insight or ability we don't know about. Should we listen more closely when they make their next prediction?"

Henry walked over to where I was standing near the window and placed a hand on each of my shoulders. His face softened by half a degree. "Look, Archbishop, I know things are getting hot. But we've seen a lot together, you and me. Remember Bosnia? Remember the Quebec revolt? Come on, man. Keep your critical thinker working, and keep on reporting. Just, whatever you do, don't snap on me, all right? The last thing GNN needs is some religious nut reporting the news."

Speculation about the greenhouse effect and the Sons of Thunder's predictions soon gave way to other concerns, such as the more immediate effects of the Black Knight impact. I spent most of the day informing myself of the physical challenges the earth faced.

The resulting tidal wave inundated the British Isles, France, and parts of Spain. Portugal was no more. The airborne shockwave was heard as far away as Ethiopia, and huge polar glaciers shattered under the assault of sound. Earthquakes toppled buildings in every major European city, and perhaps coincidentally, southern California suffered the worst quake in recorded history, with over three hundred thousand lives lost in a single day.

In one of those ironic twists of fate associated with natural disasters, the eastern seaboard of the United States suffered very little in the way of real damage. Aside from some minor flooding, that part of the world remained relatively untouched.

The same could not be said for the Atlantic Ocean itself, though. Future survey flights over the Atlantic would reveal a putrid maroon swamp of blood and animal carcasses where there used to be an ocean. Estimates of the number of fish and mammals killed by Black Knight varied widely but were all staggering. Elevated radiation levels precluded any cleanup effort, which was just as well. Most of the world's hard-core environmentalists were now a part of the death and decay the Atlantic had become, and Ariel, now disgraced, was unable to generate enough support for such a cleanup mission.

That night I dreamed.

I stood atop the Mount of Olives. The sky was gray and cloudy, and strong gusts of wind whipped around my legs and arms. I looked down at Jerusalem, where hundreds of people crowded around the Temple and where flames danced high out of the Brazen Altar in the courtyard. The people stood for long moments, gazing into the Temple as if mesmerized.

Then, with the precision of a military drill team, hundreds of right hands raised themselves toward the Temple door. A beam of light shot out of the Temple and quickly touched each hand, one after the other until they all glowed a dull red. As the light touched each hand, the people bowed low toward the Temple. After several moments, the throng stood, turned away from the Temple, and began to shout and shake their fists at the sky.

Lightning flashed. Thunder rumbled. As quickly as a flock of birds turns in mid-flight, the gathered mass on the Temple Mount doubled over, writhing in pain. Then, one by one, they each burst into flames, the fire consuming each body until only a knot of black ash remained.

After the last person burned, I heard a voice. It was a man's voice, strong and clear. I spun around to locate the speaker. Nothing but the wind. I heard him again.

"Repent," he said, "for the Lion of the tribe of Judah has triumphed, and He reigns forever."

He was above me. I looked up. Gliding effortlessly through the sky, white robes shimmering in the wind, was a powerfully-built man with angel's wings. He was a warrior with a gold chest plate, a gold cord around his waist, and a long sword in his right hand. His massive white wings altered their efforts, and he lighted five feet in front of me. His thick, brown hair came to rest on his shoulders. He looked grave, all business, but not threatening. I was at once afraid and fascinated by this person.

"Thomas Beckett," he said.

I nodded.

"This is the word of the Lord: 'There is little time. You must not take on your body the Mark of the Beast. No matter what happens, you must not.' Do you understand, Thomas Beckett?"

"I—no. What mark?"

"Believe on the Lord Jesus, who died for your sins. He will sustain you. Do not take the Mark."

Blackness.

"Thomas." Not the angel's voice, but a familiar one. "Thomas." It was Henry. "Thomas, wake up."

Merciless reality assaulted me. Lights. Camera. Action. I sat up, opened my eyes. "I'm up, I'm up," I slurred. My mouth felt like lead. I shivered reflexively as cold sweat stole too much heat from my body.

"Thomas," Henry was saying, "are you all right, Old Buddy?"

I blinked and took a deep breath before answering. "Yes. Yes, I'm fine. Just a nightmare, that's all."

"From the looks of you, I'd say the bogeyman got you this time." Henry walked back over to his bed and lay down. No daylight shone through the window.

"What time is it?" I mumbled.

"Four-thirty."

I stood and trudged to the small bathroom, turning on the light. I looked old. The chaotic salt-and-pepper mop of hair seemed to show more gray than yesterday. New lines in my forehead and around my eyes screamed at me, mocked me. Having received no encouragement from the man in the mirror, I stepped aside to the toilet and closed my eyes.

An angel. Why was I dreaming of mythical beings I did not believe in? I thought of my sister Ann. She once told me she dreamt quite often of angels. They would bring her messages, she said. Messages from God.

A dull throbbing pain emptied my chest of any other feeling. It spread outward to my shoulders and upward to the bottom of my throat, where it formed a large lump.

No. Ann is gone. Getting worked up about it serves no purpose,

and it certainly would not bring her back. <u>Why am I dreaming of angels?</u>
<u>Is God trying to communicate with me?</u> I blinked twice. The thought
had come without my permission. It was ludicrous. Why would a confirmed atheist think that God was trying to get something across through
a dream? Stress?

Ready answers are elusive at four-thirty. No voice boomed out
of the sky; there was only the incessant echo of the dream's message:
"Do not take the Mark." Whatever that meant. I could expect no help
from the face in the mirror, so I returned to bed.

Chapter 15: Shock

The day of King Joshua's assassination, members of the World Cabinet went into secret session to decide which of them would gain control of ben-David's four Earth Regions—Europe, Russia, Northern Africa, and the Middle East. There were reports of infighting which were probably true, and rumors of physical violence which were questionable. The number of guards posted inside as well as outside the meeting rooms would argue against that ever happening. Still, the fact that none of the Cabinet members had been seen for nearly three days only added fuel to the wildfire rumors.

Meanwhile, renegade China, who had yet to send a delegate to the World Cabinet since its inception, had mobilized her army. Seizing the opportunity afforded by ben-David's death, an estimated two hundred million Asian soldiers were now gathering for a huge offensive to the north and west. Various small wars broke out all over the globe as threatened and ambitious leaders struggled to increase their stock in whatever new order would arise out of the current crisis.

By day three following the assassination, the leader-less Russians were on the brink of both civil war and destruction at the hands of the Chinese. The Russian Ambassador made a frantic call to the World Cabinet Headquarters in Rome, begging for military as well as political support. No cabinet member took his call. Such is the fate of a puppet without the influence of the puppeteer.

Linda had called Henry and me back to New York. We were to catch a flight out as soon as we had reported on the official death of Joshua ben-David as the doctors turned off the machines that kept his body alive. Ben-David's scheduled demise was the only definite decision to come out of the World Cabinet's closed chambers. Like all up and coming big dogs, they wanted the old dog safely dead.

The hospital in Tel Aviv, where King ben-David had been transferred, hastily set up a room for the press conference in an unused operating room. It was stereotypically sterile-looking, with surgical green screens encircling the rows of folding chairs. Seven doctors in green scrubs and white lab coats stood facing the gathered members of the press. A tall, hairy man with slightly stooped shoulders marched into the room and stood behind the small plexiglass podium. His green cap, shoe covers, and the mask that dangled around his neck gave him the appearance of a surgeon who was between operations; he just stopped long enough to say a few words, and then he would be off to the O.R. down the hall.

"Ladies and gentlemen of the press," he began. "Today, at ten-oh-two a.m., all life-support machines attached to King Joshua ben-David were shut off. He was pronounced dead at ten-oh-three a.m."

Shouting in the hallway drew every eye to the double doors the doctor had come through moments ago.

Confusion. The voices got louder.

I jumped up and was the first to burst through the doors. Nurses, orderlies, and doctors ran down the hall toward the I.C.U.

Then I heard the words my ears refused to believe. A nurse in green scrubs ran against the flow, yelling, "He's alive! King Joshua is alive!"

Chapter 16: A Night at the Temple

Henry closed the laptop and looked up. "Well, that settles it. Linda's flying over on the SST. She'll be here early this evening."

"Linda, flying here? Why? Sure, it's a great story—"

"—the greatest."

"But we don't need her." I paced over to the window and studied the dark, angry sky that Black Knight's impact had given us. The high clouds of debris fought and rolled over each other, changing constantly with a bland sameness that was annoying at best. Pondered long enough, it became maddening. I longed to see blue sky again and wondered if I ever would.

"Of course we don't need her, but she wants to be here. You should have seen her on the video. She had tears streaming down her face, Thomas. King Joshua's resurrection isn't just big news; it's big emotionally, too."

"Yes, but tears? Linda?" I turned to face my friend. He nodded. "The Ice Queen cried, eh? Well, I guess it's what we've all been feeling. I can't think of any leader since JFK who has been better loved than King Joshua."

There was a spontaneous moment of silence as Henry thought that one over. "Can you imagine what the people's reaction would have been if Kennedy had recovered?"

"Jubilation. Mass jubilation," I said, and a very old wound reopened in my heart. "I was just a teen living in London with my parents when JFK was assassinated. Even there, thousands of miles away, I knew I had lost something. Mother cried for days. Father was suddenly spending longer hours at the office, whether by choice or necessity I don't know."

"And that's when you decided to become a reporter, right?"

"No, that's when I decided to become a plumber."

"A plumber?"

"I thought that being a reporter would be too dangerous. Plumbing was the perfect solution—great pay, great demand, and out of harm's way."

Henry leaned back in his chair and grinned. "So, Mr. Goodflush, what turned you away from that noble profession?"

I frowned and said gloomily, "I couldn't stand the smell." We both laughed for the first time in over three days.

Linda arrived at the hotel several hours later with luggage in hand. She wore an earth tone skirt and blazer and low-heeled shoes for travelling. Henry and I met her in the lobby, and I almost did not recognize her. Gone was the dour, stony-faced producer I knew. I had never met this bright, cheery little girl. I was struck with just how attractive, almost beautiful, Linda could be with the right attitude.

"Henry. Thomas. Have I missed it?"

Henry laughed easily. "No. The king doesn't speak for another hour."

"Good," she said breathlessly. "That means I have time to freshen up first. Has anyone seen him since he . . . well—"

"Recovered?" I offered. "No. The king has been in the palace with the World Cabinet all day. No one knows what they're discussing in there, but my guess is the Black Knight crisis." Henry snorted. "Henry thinks it's the Chinese military buildup."

"Hey, Archbishop, this is the first time the Emperor has been to a World Cabinet meeting. That's big news. What else could they be talking about?"

Linda looked puzzled at our rivalry over this issue, so I explained, "We have a small wager riding on this one."

"Oh," she said, eyes widening with mild amusement. "But how are you two going to settle this when the Cabinet is in closed session?"

Henry looked at me and laughed.

"We agreed," I said, feeling giddy and foolish about having agreed to such a wager, "to look at the content of his speech tonight. Whatever he talks about most is most likely what the Cabinet has been discussing."

"You goin' down, pretty boy," Henry said and laughed again.

The Temple mount is not a place to go after nightfall. With the still-present, however slight, possibility of Arab terrorism, the entire Temple Mount is off limits after dark. There is no one there but the guards, and they are likely to shoot on sight. Tonight was different.

Giant floodlights powered by portable generators illuminated the outer and inner courts of the Temple. Thousands of people from every ethnic background imaginable jostled and slithered and wove in and out in an effort to be just a little closer to the king when he appeared. Turbans, saris, and Armani suits blended into one pulsating mass of humanity.

Since Henry and I are not Jewish, we were not allowed into the walled-off inner court where the sacrificial Brazen Altar sent flames dancing into the sky. Linda, by virtue of her heritage, was somewhere inside those walls, closer than we were, but not as close as the ultra-orthodox Jewish men. These were the men who wore nothing but black and who could trace their family tree all the way back to Adam, which they inevitably did if you talked to them long enough.

"Stupid place for a press conference," I groused.

"Lighten up, Thomas. You're just mad 'cause you can't be on the front row."

"Maybe, but I still don't like reporting the news from a mile away."

"You're exaggerating."

"Not by much. At least Linda was able to get an aerial drone camera." I looked up, and even though the sky was dark I had no trouble locating the tiny automated GNN blimp that held the video and audio equipment. "I would hate to see what would happen to our ratings if we had to get the footage from here."

"You can gripe all you want," said Henry, breathing deeply the night air, "but this is just the right place. Think, Thomas . . . the man died and lived to tell about it. The Temple is the perfect place for his official resurrection. Just the right mixture of religion and political importance."

Maybe I was just being a grouch, I reasoned. What Henry said made sense. The king knew what he was doing. I decided to put aside my complaints about our working conditions.

The air around me crackled with anticipation, and with good reason. Not only was it a relief to have the Man of Peace back in the arena of world politics where he belonged, but the Israeli hope in ben-David as their Messiah seemed suddenly justified. The Hebrew scriptures that foretell a Messiah in the family tree of David who would reign forever now seemed plausible, even likely, to be fulfilled.

If killing Joshua ben-David did not stop him, nothing would.

That mysterious statement from my interview with Ezra ben-Hadad, the High Priest, came vividly to mind: "At this moment, only King ben-David and I know how this will happen." He was talking about how King Joshua could reign forever. My mind reeled with the implications of that statement. Could ben-Hadad and ben-David have possibly known ahead of time that the king would be assassinated? And if they knew, why didn't they prevent it? But if they had known, and had prevented it, then the king would not have been assassinated and could not have come back to life. So if they knew, then they must have—

I was jolted from this maddening train of thought by Henry's elbow in my rib cage.

"Hey, Archbishop," he said with a grin, "how long will it take for the two party crashers to show up this time? Place your bets now. Twenty bucks says five minutes, tops."

"Come, now, my prince," I said, feigning offense. "They've never taken much more than five minutes. You'll have to give me more breathing space if you want a chance at my money."

"All right then, I'll give them three minutes or less from the time ben-David begins his speech. Any more than that and you win."

"Done," I said.

"Three minutes," he mumbled. "I can't believe I agreed to three minutes. You're a thief and a scoundrel, Thomas Beckett. You know that, don't you?"

"Henry, I believe that is the nicest thing you've said to me all day."

"Yeah, well don't count on it getting any better. Especially if you win that bet."

Henry and I managed to muscle our way to within feet of the gate that led into the Temple court. From where we were standing, we could see directly in front of us the large Brazen altar. Beyond that were the steps leading up to the Temple itself. Ben-David had ordered that the Temple be rebuilt using the plans the Hebrew scriptures record Yahweh gave Solomon for the first Temple. This decision had caused a minor stir among Orthodox Jews who felt that the Temple described in the 40th chapter of book of Ezekiel should be built instead. Once the ancient measurements were translated into their modern equivalent, though, it was discovered that the Temple specified in that plan would be too large to fit on the Temple Mount, and the older plans were accepted without further argument. Using Solomon's plans and the newly-discovered location of the first Temple, the Israeli builders had built in record time a breathtaking edifice. Many hailed it as the "eighth man-made wonder of the world."

It faced east, with the front gate in a direct line between the entrance to the Temple proper and the sealed Eastern Gate on the Temple Mount. Had it not been for the glare of the sacrificial flames arcing and dancing before us, we would have from where we were standing been able to see into the Holy Place—the interior of the Temple itself—all the way to the final curtain that hid the Most Holy Place. This was the square room that now held the long-lost Ark of the Covenant, the most precious and sought-after treasure of antiquity—the gold-overlaid box that contained the Presence of the God of Israel.

A figure dressed in traditional rabbinical robes emerged from the Temple. A reverent hush fell over those gathered inside the Temple court. I knew it was Ezra ben-Hadad, the High Priest, even before I reached for the tiny set of binoculars I always carried in my suit coat for times like this. Ben-Hadad descended the steps, and the crowd looked like a marching band as they parted to make room for the High Priest to walk to the Brazen Altar. The closer he came to the altar, the more general the silence became until he ascended the steps and only a few scattered whispers could be heard.

"Children of Abraham," he began, "and Children of the earth. Today we have seen with our own eyes the most powerful miracle God ever wrought in Israel." He raised his arm and gestured to a point high and behind me. "Behold! Your Savior approaches."

Seemingly suspended over the Eastern Gate, arms spread wide, was the shape of a man. Two spotlights suddenly illuminated Joshua ben-David hovering in mid-air. He began to descend, floating toward the Temple.

I used my binoculars to search for the wires that held him. Not only were there no wires, there was no crane or any other machine visible that could have held a man aloft. I listened. No rush of air from a jet pack, only the astonished gasp of the spectators.

The spotlights and the GNN drone camera tracked his movements as ben-David floated gracefully less than ten feet above the heads of the people outside the Temple court. He came closer, and I muttered, "Would you look at that," just as the king swooped over our heads and entered the inner court.

He hovered momentarily over the altar, and its flames flickered and danced beneath him. As he descended, the huge flames died down until they were no more, and Joshua ben-David stood on the edge of the altar, bathed in spotlights. People nearest the altar shrank away in fear. Even I was alarmed at ben-David's unusual entrance and the fire's sudden and unnatural death.

"Children of Israel," his voice boomed, "fear not." He paused. People stopped shrinking back and instead moved forward, drawn to this most unusual man as surely as if they had been caught in a fisherman's net and were being pulled into a boat. There was something irresistible about him; he exuded confidence and excitement. At the sound of his voice, fear was replaced by expectancy. "Fear not," he repeated. "Messiah has come, and he will reign on David's throne forever."

A cheer rose from within and without the walls of the Temple court that was so loud that I thought the walls themselves might crumble. Henry and I were no different from anyone else. It was the most amazing thing. Our king—back from the dead!

Sociologists have studied for years the dynamics of large groups. They call it "mob mentality." But this was a feeling and a phenomenon as far removed from mob mentality as is a nuclear explosion from a slap in the face. In an instant, each and every one of us had become ben-David's subject, to do with as he pleased. He could have told any one of us to kill or to die for him, and there would have been no hesitations, no questions asked.

The roar lasted several minutes, with ben-David walking around the altar, empowered by the adoration, basking in the warmth of our love. When the cheers finally subsided, he continued, "As it is written in the book of the prophet Isaiah: 'the government shall be upon his shoulder'" Thousands of voices within and without the wall joined him in a chant-like recitation of the remainder. "'And his name shall be called Wonderful, Counsellor, The mighty God, The everlasting Father, The Prince of Peace.'" The king paused and surveyed his loyal subjects. A sense of awe filled our hearts as the implications of those words sank in. Then ben-David smiled and said, "Today this prophecy is fulfilled."

I wonder now that I did not go deaf in the minutes following that statement.

King ben-David turned and descended the steps of the Brazen altar, and the crowd parted; some men I could see were bowing as they made room for the king. He ascended the steps to the Temple and, reaching the top, turned to face his subjects.

Joshua held his hands high in the air, and the cheers subsided. He said, "Now it is time for me to take my rightful place as king and priest over Israel and the world. Children of Israel, we now have a global society and a global faith. I have come to proclaim that all the children of the world are Abraham's seed. I have come as the completion of all the Law and the Prophets require. No longer will you sacrifice animals and grain offerings. From now until forever, you will bring the wealth of the nations to me."

Another general shout. The high priest, all but forgotten since the king had made his entrance, came forward out of the crowd and climbed the Temple steps. Reaching the top, he prostrated himself before the king until all we could see of the high priest was a cloak draped over a lump on the paving stones. After a moment, ben-David reached down and touched ben-Hadad's shoulder. Israel's high priest stood, and leaning over slightly, ben-David spoke into his ear. Ben-Hadad nodded and turned to face the assembled masses.

He said, "In ancient times, God spoke to Moses and commanded him to build the Ark of the Covenant, so that God's Name would have a home, and God's Spirit would go with the Israelites wherever they went. Since that time, the Spirit of ben-David has rested on that Ark, but now that he is here, his Spirit no longer resides in an Ark, and we know his Name. Now he lives with us, and from now until forever, his Name will rest in the Most Holy Place. Children of the world, behold the spirit and image of your God and king!"

Ben-Hadad stepped back so that he no longer stood in front of the entrance to the Temple, and as if on cue, the curtain that separated the Holy Place from the Most Holy Place in the back of the Temple crumpled to the ground. The inside of the Temple was illuminated with a golden glow, and even though I was outside the court yard, I had no trouble seeing the newest addition to the Temple furnishings, even without my tiny binoculars. A gold statue of Joshua ben-David dressed in royal robes and wearing a crown stood at the back of the Temple. It was about forty feet tall—almost as tall as the building itself. Slowly, I brought the binoculars up to my eyes.

I was struck with a reverent awe, but a voice from somewhere in the dark corners of my mind screamed out that this was all wrong. The Most Holy Place was meant for the Ark of the Covenant only. This was a place so holy to the Israelis that, historically, only the high priest was allowed to even look behind that curtain. The curtain itself was so heavy it seemed to be more like a wall than anything else. Now, to see the curtain, the "veil" as the Hebrews call it, come down with no warning was a blow so great I winced. How would the religious Jews react to this newest development?

Then the statue moved.

It was almost imperceptible at first, and if I had not been using magnification, I would have missed it. It was as though the whole statue expanded momentarily and then contracted again, almost as if it were taking the first breath of life. I joined in the collective gasp that came from those closest to the Temple.

"What?" Henry said. "What's happening, Thomas?"

I was about to answer him when we felt the stones under our feet rumble and heard a grating sound, like the sound of two cement blocks being rubbed together, magnified ten thousand times. The image of ben-David took a step forward, and even those who had not reacted to the monument's first movement now reacted with shock. One question was etched on every face: "What is going on?" The statue took another step and was at the entrance to the Temple. The ground beneath me stirred again.

Now in the same light that had brightened ben-David's aerial entrance, this image could not be discounted as an illusion or a trick. I studied its texture, shape, and movements. It was no robot—there were no mechanical joints in the limbs. It was living, moving metal. I had never in thirty-five years of reporting the news seen anything like it, nor have I since.

Then, as if things were not already strange enough, the statue addressed those present as well as the remote cameras with a charisma echoing that of the real Joshua ben-David. "Citizens of earth," it began in a voice that rumbled like distant thunder. "You have now seen with your own eyes your Messiah-king raised from the dead."

Just like the woman outside my apartment in New York. And just like the teenager in the accident in Tennessee. The thoughts came unbidden.

"He has conquered the final foe."

So did the Essene preacher. And Ann. They raised those people from the dead with a few words. Another spontaneous association. Where was my subconscious leading me? Should I not be impressed by someone being raised from the dead just because it has been done before? I told my subconscious to shut up.

"Joshua ben-David is victorious!" the statue concluded. At that, we all cheered as one, with every hand being raised into the air at the same moment in a gesture of victory and celebration.

Even over our loudest shouts, the image of ben-David made its voice heard. "Is anyone like Joshua ben-David? He alone has brought peace to the earth. He alone is god over the earth. Now give him the reverence and honor he deserves."

We looked to the real ben-David, dwarfed in size by the talking statue, but now appearing to us more radiant than ever. Spontaneously, everyone bowed, including the high priest and the image. The native Israelis, including nearly all of those who were inside the Temple court, prostrated themselves in true Middle-Eastern fashion, curling up on the ground with their noses touching the pavement stones. Henry and I and other Westerners contented ourselves with dropping to one or two knees and bowing our heads.

I have no recollection of how long we were in that state. The only clue I had to the passage of time was the rhythmic ebb and flow of the voices of the assembled, like ocean waves alternately crashing loudly onto the shore and receding quietly into the sea. It was as if a spell had been cast—had I wanted to move, I would have been unable. After what seemed like only a few minutes but was probably much more, the tide of adulation slowly went back out to sea. I raised my head along with the majority of the worshipers.

King Joshua crossed over to his likeness and whispered in its ear. The statue stood and said, "It is right for you to praise your king. Now there is one thing he requires of you, of each and every citizen of earth."

We silently begged it to tell us what that requirement was.

"No longer will you claim to be an Israeli or an Arab or a European or an American. The king has decreed that you are all now only to be called citizens of planet earth. He therefore abolishes all national borders and sovereignties. The members of the World Cabinet will remain in their current positions as advisers to the king, who is now Lord over all."

After the shouts of praise died down, it continued, "In order to finally unify the economies of the world, King Joshua has declared the subdermal debit card to be the new world economic standard. Every man and woman who is independent of the parental household must have a subdermal card implanted—"

"Silence."

They appeared literally out of nowhere. To this day I am unsure just how the Sons of Thunder were able to make their entrance without anyone seeing them, but there they were, one on either side of the talking statue. A cacophony of murmurs arose, ranging in emotion from angry to shocked to fearful.

Henry uttered an expletive. "They're late."

The memory of our bet struggled to the surface as a tempest of questions and possibilities swept through my mind.

I was angry at the intrusion on what was possibly a turning point in the history of humankind. I was confused by these two men, and that only added to my fury. How did these arrogant, camel-hair-clad, self-righteous, self-styled prophets pull it off? They did whatever they wanted, whenever they wanted, unchallenged. They had no regard for the greatest leader this world had ever known, confronting him with baseless allegations and prophecies of doom. How could they—what gave them the right?

I firmly decided then that King Joshua should have them killed, and having decided, I allowed myself to comment on the triviality of my bet with Henry. "Pay up," I said.

"Yeah," Henry said, "right after I get my subdermal."

During the several seconds since the appearance of the Sons of Thunder, no one on the Temple porch had moved. The statue was silent and still, now looking more like a carved piece of gold than the moving, breathing apparition that had only moments ago amazed us all with its oration. The real King Joshua regarded the new arrivals with a regal calmness that bordered on arrogance.

James slowly walked around the king and then addressed the Jews within the court yard. "Sons of Abraham, how has this man bewitched you? With tricks of levitation, with an idol that speaks? And now you are ready to exchange the God of your fathers for a statue of gold and a covenant with Satan." That got a reaction. Though he was not speaking to me, I was nearly as offended as the Orthodox Jews. James was cheapening what I had seen, mocking my perception of reality.

John crossed in front of the statue. "To the Law and the Prophets! Is this not the abomination Daniel spoke of?" he shouted, gesturing over his shoulder to the statue. "Hear the word of the Lord: 'Anyone who enters into a covenant with this man and his image will also bear on his body the mark of My wrath. You will be afflicted with sores; painful boils will break out all over your bodies. You will seek relief but will find none—this is the judgment on those who follow the wicked shepherd and the abomination he has set up.'"

There was a sudden shift in the atmosphere. A groundswell of murmurs arose. Many of us who were so amazed by the talking statue were now confused. Henry leaned over and said, "Abomination? What's he talking about?"

I tried to speak and, realizing that my mouth was hanging open, closed it and paused to construct my answer. "I don't know," was all I could muster.

I stepped back mentally and made an effort to be objective as the Sons of Thunder ranted on about the judgment of boils and the wrath of God.

Joshua ben-David had in a few minutes' time either abolished or radically changed many traditions that the Hebrew nation had held for thousands of years. That in itself was an amazing accomplishment. No other culture in the history of the world has been able to preserve traditions like the descendants of Abraham. Through dozens of generations of exile, hardship, slavery, brutality, and near-extinction, they have held on to the rituals and customs that make them a people.

Now they were willing to either modify or discard those beliefs at the whim of this man named Joshua. Before today, no one dared mention to an Orthodox Jew that anything other than the Ark of the Covenant belonged in the Most Holy Place. Now, a golden statue—an idol—had been seen and accepted by the most orthodox Jews imaginable—the Levitical priesthood.

I watched the group of priests closest to the Temple steps through my binoculars as James and John pled their case. The two self-proclaimed prophets spoke with more fiery passion than I had ever seen, quoting the Hebrew scriptures as if they had written them. Their fervent oration began to have an effect. Jewish priests began to whisper to each other and gesture excitedly. It seemed to me that the Sons of Thunder were beginning to sway most of them.

James concluded, "Will you cut a covenant with the one who has desecrated the house of the Lord? Brothers, listen to me—these are the days of Jacob's Trouble. The judgment of God is now poured out, and who can stand? Run!" he yelled. "Run to the mountains. Let the God of Abraham, Isaac, and Jacob protect you from this wicked king." He pointed at ben-David, who had just returned from conferring with one of his aides. Rage contorted the king's face, but he said nothing. Then, just as suddenly as they had appeared, James and John vanished. A rush of wind and a dull twin thud and they were gone. It was almost as if they had never been there.

King ben-David's face calmed gradually. Finally, he began, "Children of Israel—" That was enough to break the spell of shock.

Run.

Those closest to the Temple tried hardest to be the first ones out of the city. Henry and I ducked to the side and pressed our backs against the wall just in time to avoid being crushed by the fleeing masses. I heard screams and shouts as dozens of people were trampled in the flight. Those outside the Temple court were slower to react, serving as an impenetrable wall of humanity impeding the escape of those inside. It was all the opportunity ben-David needed.

"Stop," he said calmly, and his voice was amplified more than before. It boomed out across the Temple Mount.

With my back against the wall, I could no longer see Joshua ben-

David; I saw faces. Thousands of faces of every shape, size, and color. But with all that variety—each face different from every other face—I was struck with how much alike they looked. They shared an expression, one that I had seen before on dozens of brainwashed cult members. It was a look of total subjection, total devotion, like a favorite dog looks when his master comes home. These people, thousands of them, had been sucked into the vortex of King Joshua's charisma. Add to that his being raised from the dead, and they would follow him to their own funerals.

Caught between escapees and devotees, I found myself at a crossroads. Was I looking in a mirror? I always tried to remain objective, but hadn't I bowed to the king along with everyone else?

What was wrong with me? I closed my eyes tightly. A scene flashed across my mind. A view from the Mount of Olives. Thousands bowing before the Temple. The angel. The dream. I shut my eyes tightly, trying to separate reality from fantasy. The problem was, reality was beginning to look more and more like fantasy all the time.

Don't take the mark. The words of the angel pounded inside my mind. James' voice added a chorus of its own. A covenant with Satan. My shout of frustration went unheard in the chaos that reigned on the Temple Mount.

Gradually, that chaos abated as the calming influence of King Joshua's voice took effect. Those who had not been trampled and still wished to leave were allowed to go. Medical teams were called in to care for the injured. Joshua ben-David continued speaking, and within half an hour he had removed all the fears and doubts instilled by the visit of the Sons of Thunder.

As ben-David left to the sound of uproarious applause, he touched his statue and it again animated itself and returned to its place at the back of the Temple. Ezra ben-Hadad concluded the evening with details of how everyone on planet earth was to report to one of the many "Subdermal Stations" as soon as possible to receive his or her new debit card.

After Linda rejoined us, we returned to the hotel. It was two o'clock in the morning, but unlike Henry, I was too keyed up to go straight to bed. I sat in a chair and stared out the window.

I have never been a believer in dreams, but what happened that night on the Temple Mount looked too much like my dream to ignore it or pass it off as mere coincidence. And then there were the messages from the angel and from the Sons of Thunder. Dream and reality. They used different words, but the message was the same—Don't do what the king wants. What did it all mean?

All right, Thomas, time to think like a reporter. Find the link. I flipped up the screen of the laptop and waited for it to go through its boot process.

The keywords were "mark" and "covenant." They were related in that I was not supposed to accept either one. "Mark" was too vague, so I began with "covenant." I was familiar with the word in its definition as a contract, but as I read through the Web database on this word, things became clearer.

In ancient times, and even in some modern cultures, a covenant was more than a mere contract. It was and is a blood-sworn oath, pure and inviolate. Reading on, I discovered that this type of agreement is so serious that anyone entering into a blood covenant would rather die than break that agreement. And in the cultures that practice it, homicide of covenant-breakers is more than commonplace—it is an unyielding law. Whole families will hunt and kill a brother or a daughter or a cousin if that person is guilty of breaking a covenant.

The procedure for initiating a covenant varies from culture to culture, but I noticed some common features. First, there was the reading or recitation of the conditions of the covenant. These conditions usually involved the complete identification of one person or tribe with another—what is mine is yours, and vice-versa.

Then there was the shedding of blood. Each person, or a representative of each group, would cut himself on the hand or arm and allow the blood to drain into a cup or bowl. The blood of the two parties would be mixed together, symbolizing the complete identification of one with the other. What they did with the blood after that varied somewhat. Some added a beverage and drank it, some used the blood as an ornament or face paint. But one aspect of this part of the ritual screamed out at me from the laptop monitor.

Instead of bandaging these cuts, the covenant partners would rub ashes or gun powder or dirt into the wounds so that there would be a lasting and highly visible scar. The covenant-keeper carried the mark of that covenant for the rest of his life.

That was the connection. The mark and the covenant are one, and I was being told not to participate in either one.

Chapter 17: The Covenant

As Henry, Linda, and I walked along the narrow streets of Jerusalem, I wondered at the sheer number of people out and about. It was to be expected, I suppose, since we were all being required to obtain a subdermal debit card as soon as possible. Ironically, the atmosphere on the streets was convivial, almost joyous. There was no hint that anyone had given any consideration or credence to the words spoken by the Sons of Thunder the night before, or that they had even remembered them. We were all going to obtain our subdermal debit cards, and we would all be unified as global citizens in a global economy under the smiling eyes of Joshua ben-David.

The government of King Joshua ben-David was not about to let anyone forget to get his or her subdermal debit card. I had never seen an advertising campaign this extensive. Flyers, television commercials, signs on buses, and billboards were omnipresent. They all had the same message: "The subdermal debit cards are here. Get yours today."

The Eurobank ads proclaimed their financial gospel at every corner and in every language. Some of them had catchy, cryptic messages suitable for pop culture consumption. My personal favorite was the sign that showed a picture of Joshua ben-David lovingly gazing at a basketball-sized earth hovering over his outstretched right hand. Beams of light shot from his palm upward, illuminating the globe and his face. The caption read: "A world of opportunity."

In order to accommodate everyone as quickly as possible, Eurobank had set up subdermal stations everywhere. One could hardly walk half a mile in any direction without seeing at least one or two of the hastily-constructed tents. Even so, there were lines at all of them.

As we approached the next one, I began to abandon hope that we would find a subdermal station with a short line. Linda must have read my mind, for she said, "Well, gentlemen, shall we wait in line here or look for greener pastures?"

"We're in Israel in the midst of a drought," I said. "There are no greener pastures."

Having arrived at the back of the line, I observed some of those exiting the tent with gauze bandages on their right hands. Most of their faces displayed their discomfort. Anesthetic was evidently in short supply. An elderly man whose right arm and leg had been amputated hobbled out of the tent on one crutch. He wore a bandage on his forehead. He appeared less disturbed by the procedure than the others, but he looked as though he had survived much worse.

Jabbing a thumb in the old man's direction, Henry said, "That must be Plan B."

The procedure was swift, so it took less time to reach the registration table than I had imagined. Two women and one man sat at the table behind stacks of forms and cups filled with pens. Henry, Linda, and I approached the table simultaneously. The fresh-faced Israeli woman handed me a form and a pen.

"Please sign and date on the bottom line, then step behind the curtain," she said in flat officialese.

"What's this?" I said.

"That is your Covenant. A mere formality."

"May I read it first," I said, not as a question. Henry stopped scanning his Covenant form and rolled his eyes. My firm read-carefully-before-signing-anything conviction had always annoyed the more impulsive Henry II, but then, it was not his name I was to sign.

The woman's frank gesture indicated that I should step aside if I wanted to indulge my compulsion. I obliged. In spite of his usual impulsiveness, Henry stepped out of line with me. Linda quickly scanned and signed her Covenant form and disappeared behind the privacy curtain.

I grinned at Henry. "Don't tell me that after all these years working with me you're finally learning something."

"Naw, man, it's not you—it was that truckload of furniture I didn't know I'd bought last year."

"Ah, I see." I nodded and began reading the Covenant form. After skimming through two paragraphs of fine-print legalese, I read:

> I, the undersigned, hereby affirm that I am now a Citizen of Earth, owing no allegiance to any national power, sovereignty, king, or god, but only to Planet Earth and to the established government, to wit: the World Cabinet. Further, I affirm and identify myself with the institutions, laws, religion, and governance of our God and king Joshua ben-David.

More legal mumbo-jumbo for three-quarters of a page, and then this final paragraph:

Let this document serve as witness that if the undersigned Citizen of Earth should ever break the Covenant established herein, he or she shall be given over to the courts, and shall have land and property confiscated and shall be imprisoned or tortured or executed as the courts shall determine.

My stomach tightened. Did I really want to do this? This document went beyond a simple contract. It was a covenant. My hand began to quiver slightly. This paper was a life-and-death proposition.

What if I didn't want to be a "Citizen of Earth?" What if at some point I decide I disagree with ben-David's politics or his religion? According to this document, he would have every legal right to have me executed.

The fact that the so-called minor operation to implant the subdermal card involved an incision, blood, and a lasting scar did little to allay my fears.

"Man, this is weird," Henry mumbled.

"Weird? It's frightening."

"No, I mean I had this dream."

"A dream?"

"Yeah. I was right here. Just like this, and this—this angel flew down out of the sky and told me not to sign the paper."

"Angel? What did it look like?"

"That was the strange part. Dude was about seven feet tall. A brother, real dark. With dreads."

A black angel with dreadlocks? I supposed that would be no more unusual or surreal than my warrior angel.

"What did he say?"

"I don't remember, exactly," Henry said. "I've been trying to forget it. Something about don't sign, don't take the mark—that's it, don't take the mark."

"Let's go back to the hotel. I have something to show you."

"What about Linda?"

As if on cue, Linda Friedman emerged from behind the curtain with a gauze bandage on her right hand. She cradled it in her left and studied the bandage as she walked. The tightness in my stomach doubled. Not paying attention to where she was going, she almost bumped into Henry before noticing we were there.

"Oh. Where have you guys been? I'm already finished."

"Linda," I said, "did you read that form before you signed it?"

"Well, no, not really. It seemed like pretty standard stuff."

I handed her my form and pointed out the two key paragraphs. She was unmoved. I said, "Don't you have a problem with signing away your American freedoms just like that?"

"Thomas, freedom is an illusion. It's relative to your viewpoint. King Joshua has brought peace and security to our world. To me, that is more liberating than anything the Constitution ever gave me."

"And you are willing to die for King Joshua and what he stands for."

She thought for a moment and then nodded. "Yes, Thomas, I am."

Back at the hotel, I called up my covenant research on the laptop for Henry to read. Linda was not interested and had gone straight back to her room, claiming a headache. After Henry had read the information on covenants, I told him about my dream and about how closely it paralleled the events on the Temple Mount the night before.

Henry let out a low whistle. "I didn't think it was possible, but your dream has mine beat for weirdness. Now that we know the subdermals are bad news, I just have one question."

"Oh?"

"The statue said we have to get them—how we gonna avoid it?"

When the Sons of Thunder made their next appearance, Henry and I were just finishing lunch. We received an anonymous phone call from one of ben-David's staff, and Henry and I rushed to the Temple mount to cover their latest rantings.

Before we left, I had knocked on Linda's door to tell her where we were going, but she declined to go with us. Through the closed door she told me that her headache was worse than it had been earlier. She sounded depressed. I told her to take some pain medication and get better.

The two prophets were saying basically the same things they had the night before when they interrupted Joshua ben-David's ceremony. They reminded us of their earlier pronouncement that anyone entering into ben-David's covenant would break out in boils, and they said that even now, some already were afflicted with this disorder. I had yet to see boils on anyone in the city, but I thought about Linda and worried.

Then James made another pronouncement. He said that since so many were making a blood covenant with the wicked king, God would give us blood to drink. Henry scoffed, but I was not as eager to laugh at men whose every word came true.

We returned to the hotel to find a note from the management informing us that due to the drought, water rationing was being initiated throughout the city. Some common-sense rules for water conservation were included, along with a reminder to hurry and get our subdermals by the end of the week, or we might have problems paying our hotel bill.

I called Linda's room to check on her, but there was no answer. I walked over and knocked on the door. She did not answer, but I could hear quiet sobs through the thin walls.

"Linda?" No answer. "Linda, I hear you crying."

"Go away, Beckett."

"Linda, what's wrong?" Henry now stood beside me, concern creasing his forehead.

"Nothing. I just want to be left alone."

"Linda," Henry said, "isn't there something we can do for you?" The sobs grew louder, closer.

I said, "Linda, you know us well enough to realize we're not going to leave you alone until you tell us what is wrong."

"I know. You two should brace yourselves."

The door opened. What we saw was hardly Linda. It was wearing a nightshirt and was obviously female, but nothing else about it resembled Global News Tonight producer Linda Friedman. Mountainous sores jutted from every square inch of visible flesh, grossly deforming her face, arms, legs, and even the figure she had for years so zealously protected with diet and exercise was distorted. Each sore was at least three inches in diameter, red and filled with fluid. Several had burst and were draining yellow-white pus down her arms and legs.

Henry and I cursed in unison, then I said, "What happened?"

Her tears began afresh and she shrugged, palms outward in the most helpless posture I had ever see her assume. A sore on her right shoulder broke open, and the fluid drained down her arm into her upturned hand, where the new subdermal scar was plainly visible as an oddly-shaped scab.

Chapter 18: Blood

The next morning, I awoke before sunrise in a cold sweat. I had lived through a re-run of my angel dream. I sat on the edge of the bed and ran shaking fingers through wet hair. OK, OK, I get the picture, I mentally screamed. I stumbled to the bathroom without turning on any lights. A vaguely familiar smell greeted me as I and shut the door. I relieved myself in the dark and tried to place the heavy, oppressive odor that was unlike anything Henry or I would leave behind.

I flushed the toilet and began to wash my hands. The water felt odd—oily and thick. The smell became stronger, and I made the connection. It was the smell of death and blood on the battlefield following Ezekiel's War.

I flipped the light on with my wrist. My hands were covered in blood. I gasped.

Crimson specks inside the sink joined to create droplets of blood that ran down the drain. The faucet poured out red in a steady stream. I turned the water off and back on. Hot, cold, it was all the same. The toilet bowl was filled with the viscous substance.

I dried my hands on a white hotel towel. When I hung it on the towel rack, it made the bathroom look like a murder scene.

I woke Henry with difficulty, but Linda was awake, not having slept all night. Her boils seemed even more numerous than before, and her eyes drooped with fatigue and despair. She had aged thirty years in one night and was unmoved by the news of the water that had turned to blood. The miserably ill can be surprisingly apathetic about significant events.

We reported the story, but we really should not have bothered. All over the world, the situation was the same. Reservoirs, lakes, and rivers had all turned into blood, or at least something that looked, smelled, and tasted like blood.

Once again, the Sons of Thunder had been right.

King Joshua ben-David decided that day that he had had enough and began to speak out against James and John and what they were doing. He called it a "ministry of death," and referred to the Sons of Thunder as "enemies of earth." He called upon all his loyal subjects to make it their mission in life to destroy these two men and to curse their god, "who has control over these disasters."

Ben-David explained that though he was God, there was another god with whom he had been at war for all eternity. It was this cruel god who was striking ben-David's servants with infectious sores and was turning water into blood. He called on us as citizens of earth to unite our spiritual strength with his to combat this menace. Together we would defeat the enemy.

Battle lines were being drawn, but on which side did Thomas Beckett stand? I had to decide, and soon.

Later that afternoon, Linda called Henry to her room for a conference, and he returned looking like a teen whose parents had taken away his car keys.

"What was that all about?" I asked.

"Subdermals."

"Well?"

"I'm going to get mine today."

"No."

"Look, Thomas, I know what you're gonna say. You're gonna to talk about the Covenant form and your research and my dream and your dream and Linda's boils and any other reason you can think of not to get a subdermal. But none of that matters."

"What do you mean, 'none of that matters'? It matters a great deal. This is your life and your health we are talking about."

"You're right. It's my life we're talking about, not yours. Thomas, I'm going to lose my career if I don't do this. Linda will fire me, and I'll be blackballed from every news network in the world. Man, I won't be able to get a job flippin' burgers if I don't do what she says."

"But Henry, you and I both know better. There is something seriously wrong with the subdermals. Is there any way you can put this off—at least until we can learn more about them and what's causing all these people to get sick?"

Henry answered with silence. The phone rang.

"Yes?" I said as I picked up the phone. I knew my irritation seeped over into my voice, but I did not care.

"Thomas." It was Linda. My heart skipped half a beat. "Come over to my room as soon as you can."

Chapter 19: Heaven and Earth

Henry was gone when I returned to the suite. I first cursed him for his weakness in bowing to Linda's will. Then I cursed myself for my weakness in not telling Linda where she could stuff her precious news anchor job.

But the fact was that I liked my job. I did not want to lose it over a signed paper and a minor operation. Moreover, Linda had explained that in less than a week, the transition in Israel to the new system would be complete, and no one without a subdermal debit card would be able buy or sell anything. The rest of the world would follow suit within a few weeks. I would be an economic outcast.

I had been secure in my convictions against the subdermals when I entered Linda's room, but now I found myself doubting. The research, the dream, the words of James and John and Linda and the statue all attacked my mind in a cacophony of confusion.

I sat on the edge of the bed with my head in my hands, wishing the answer would just fall out of the sky. "Oh, God," I said, and I jumped when the sound met my ears. What had begun in my mind as an expletive emerged as something more akin to a prayer. But that was silly.

Like any good atheist, I tried not to think of God. I found it much easier to believe in things I could see. I could trust a computer for information, an airplane for transportation, or myself to earn a living. I never had felt the need for a god's help, nor had I the desire to give up any portion of my life for the benefit of a god whose existence could not be proven.

"Superstition and fairy tales," I muttered. I rubbed my eyes and forced myself to think about the problem at hand. I was not comfortable with the idea of getting a subdermal. Yet if I refused, that would be the end of my career, my life as I knew it, and that option was not acceptable. When I looked at the situation from that angle, it became obvious I really had no choice.

"Thomas, old boy," I said to the empty room, "covenant or no, it looks like you will be making a trip to the nearest subdermal station." I stood and started toward the door, but my feet would not move. It felt as though my shoes had been glued to the floor. Reaching down and grabbing my legs, I grunted and strained, but they refused to budge.

With one final yank, I lost my balance and fell on my side. I almost said "Oh God," again, but I stopped the words before they could escape my mouth. But there it was again, even if only in my mind—the beginnings of a prayer.

So if it was a prayer I was starting, to whom was I praying? Joshua ben-David? I hardly thought so. He was impressive, and he did things I had never seen before, but God? Try as I might, I could not digest that concept.

I found myself once again entertaining the notion of the existence of a real god, somewhere. Perhaps I had been wrong all these years. What was it Hamlet said? <u>There are more things in heaven and earth, Horatio / Than are dreamt of in your philosophy</u>. Objectively, I had to admit the possibility that there might be a god, but practically, I had never allowed one to be "dreamt of" in my philosophy. Until now.

Then it caught my eye. Sitting on the nightstand by the bed. A Bible, placed by the Gideons, the cover proclaimed. I was sure it had not been there this morning when I awoke. Had Henry found and read it? I chuckled. <u>Right</u>.

I reached for the book, then withdrew my hand. What had I to do with a dusty collection of myths and fables? I was willing to concede that there might be a god, but I doubted that ultimate truth could be found from one source. And even if there were some truth to the old Bible legends, they would benefit me not one bit. I had real problems.

But no answers.

As if in rebellion to my rational mind, my hand shot out and grabbed the book. As soon as I touched the cover, memories of Ann flooded my mind. She had adored this book. Despite all the hardship and heartache she endured as a pastor's wife, she had remained ecstatic about her devotion to her God and her Bible.

"Annie," I whispered. "Did you know something I don't know?" I threw my last shred of rationality to the wind and opened the book somewhere near the middle.

I began reading about a bizarre dream that someone named Daniel had. For some reason, the name Daniel sounded familiar. The dream itself was incomprehensible, but I was drawn into it because, like my dream, there was an angel in Daniel's dream. An angel named Gabriel.

<u>And he said, Behold, I will make thee know what shall be in the last end of the indignation: for at the time appointed the end shall be.</u>

I was hooked. Gabriel continued with an explanation of the symbolic significance of the animals in Daniel's dream. They represented future governments as a backdrop for the real meat of the dream—the end of the world.

> And in the latter time of their kingdom, when the transgressors are come to the full, a king of fierce countenance shall stand up. And his power shall be mighty, but not by his own power . . . he shall cause deceit to prosper in his hand; and he shall magnify himself in his heart, and by peace shall destroy many: he shall also stand up against the Prince of princes; but he shall be broken without human power.

I could not shake the feeling that I was reading Joshua ben-David's dossier. Incredible. These words were written thousands of years ago. How could they possibly have anything to do with the present day? I scanned for other references to this "king of fierce countenance." I did not have to go far, only to Daniel's next vision.

> And he shall confirm the covenant with many for one week: and in the midst of the week he shall cause the sacrifice and the oblation to cease, and for the overspreading of abominations he shall make it desolate, even until the consummation.

The abomination Daniel spoke of. That was what the Sons of Thunder had called ben-David's statue, and that was why Daniel's name struck a familiar chord. James and John obviously believed this to be the time of the end, and they evidently believed ben-David to be this king. The parallels were inescapable. King ben-David had ended the very sacrificial system he had helped reinstate three and a half years ago. He had placed a statue—an idol—in the Temple. And that is a practice orthodox Judaism has never accepted as kosher.

I read that paragraph again and wondered about the people who left the Temple after James and John's appearance. If this was a description of ben-David I held in my hands, those men and women were in grave danger.

My jaw hung slack in disbelief. Up to a few minutes ago, I had always thought that Revelation, the final book in the Bible, was the only one that supposedly dealt with the end of the world. I had always scoffed at the very notion that a two-thousand-year-old book could ever predict future events. To my atheistic mind, the final book of the Christian scripture was nothing more than a collection of lunatic ravings, a case study on the effects of isolation on a senile mind. Yet, here I sat, reading a book that even predated Revelation as if it were today's headlines. Impulsively, I flipped to the back of the Bible.

Maps.

I turned a few pages the other direction, and these words captured my eyes and stopped my hands:

> After this I beheld, and, lo, a great multitude, which no man could number, of all nations, and kindreds, and people, and tongues, stood before the throne, and before the Lamb, clothed with white robes, and palms in their hands; And cried with a loud voice, saying, Salvation to our God which sitteth upon the throne, and unto the Lamb.

A sensation of warmth began at my head and worked its way down my body. I closed my eyes, and suddenly I was there, watching that scene.

Millions upon millions of people, all clothed in light, reflecting light, projecting a light all their own, covered every square foot of ground as far as I could see. But rather than a nondescript mass of humanity, each one was different; each face stood out from the rest. They were singing. They were joyful. I wanted to turn and see who was receiving this adoration, but I was unable. A voice inside my head seemed to say, "You know who."

Then, out of all those faces, I saw Ann. She looked at me and smiled. Then, without traveling the distance between us, she stood before me. She was more lovely here than in life. She radiated the same warm light everyone else did. Her hazel eyes were brighter than I remembered. Gone were the crows feet that had over the course of the past ten years permanently creased her temples, and the small dark mole she refused to have burned off her neck had been replaced by smooth, radiant skin. Her blond locks, minus the gray, fell about her shoulders in a cut I had never seen on her before. Remaining perfectly coiffed, the golden curls moved about as if blown by a gentle breeze. They seemed to take on a life of their own, speaking a language of soft, elegant motion.

"Thomas," she said and smiled. "This is where I am now. Right now. Come join me."

I started to answer, to say something, anything. She turned and skipped to the empty spot next to Pastor Bill and the boys and continued singing, hands raised.

The scene faded, and I stared at the Bible in my lap. <u>This is where I am now</u>. I mouthed the words silently four or five times.

So she was right. All these years, Ann knew and lived the truth I refused to believe. Now I was confronted with that truth and with the reality of a spiritual world I had spent my whole life trying to deny simply because I could not perceive it with my five senses. There really were stranger things in heaven and earth than were dreamt of in my philosophy. I could deny the truth no longer.

I closed the Bible, knelt beside the bed, and said, "God, you know I have not believed in You, but what You have shown me has changed my mind. I do believe You are there. I do believe the Jesus that Ann told me about was Your Son. And I also believe that James and John are Your servants.

"I don't know if there is any hope for me at this point, but Ann told me often that You would grant forgiveness and eternal life if only I repented and asked for it. I am asking now. I need You, Jesus. I—" That was all. For the next twenty minutes I cried like the newborn I was.

I was free. Free to weep. Free to laugh for no reason. Free to skip as Ann had in my vision. Free to love.

A deep, burning compassion came over me. All over the world right now, millions of people were aligning themselves irrevocably with Joshua ben-David. They were now enemies of God and would have to face His wrath because of it. I thought of how much I had in common with them. But for the decision I just made, I could be one of them—sick and cursed and doomed.

A new title for King ben-David surfaced in my mind. Antichrist: the one who is against Jesus Christ.

<u>And you are now a Christian—a "little Christ." He is just as much your enemy as he is Mine</u>.

I looked around the room. Nothing. It was my heart that had heard the voice speak in a language clearer than words.

Having King Joshua as my enemy was a sobering thought.

And what about Henry? He was probably getting his subdermal right now, if he had not already. He was entering into covenant with King ben-David. I hoped and wished and prayed that he would not.

I had just had an encounter with Jesus Christ. I now identified myself with Him, but what of my friendship with Henry—if he identified himself with ben-David, would we be able to remain friends? Henry

Wilson had been a better friend to me than any other I had ever had. I did not want to lose that friendship. I nurtured a small, quiet hope that I would somehow be able to bring Henry into a faith in Jesus Christ and save him from the wrath of God now being endured by the allies of Joshua ben-David.

A demanding fist pounded on the door to the suite. Outside, Linda said, "Beckett, are you in there? Open up."

I rose and opened the door. Linda's deformed face was distorted even further with rage. I had an immediate sense of foreboding and felt the urge to bolt, to get away from this ally of my enemy ben-David, but that voice inside me seemed to say "Stay." Linda stormed into the room, reeking of cigarette smoke, and turned to face me.

"You've been here the whole time, haven't you?"

"Whole time? I've not left the room since our little talk, if that's what you mean."

"Just what I thought. I've been calling on the phone and pounding on your door for over an hour."

"The phone has not rung. Are you sure you dialed the right number?"

"Don't be stupid. Of course I'm sure."

I closed the door slowly, noticing as I did several large wet circles where Linda had broken sores open from knocking. Evidently, she had knocked more than I had heard.

"Well, now you have my undivided attention. What can I do for you?"

"First, why haven't you gotten your subdermal yet?"

"Linda, we just talked about it—" I glanced at my watch "—an hour and a half ago. When did you think I should—"

"I don't care about that. The point is, I told you to get it, and you haven't left yet." She began pacing. "I need a cigarette. Where's Wilson?"

"Henry was gone by the time I returned. I assume he went to get his."

"Good. Now, see, there is someone who knows who fills his soup bowl. But you, you pompous, arrogant—"

The door opened and Henry walked in. His shoulders drooped, and his head hung low. Gauze covered his right palm. Small mounds of puffy flesh had already begun to make their appearance on his arms and face.

My stomach turned and my voice caught in my throat twice before I was able to say, "Henry?"

"Thomas, I'm sorry, old buddy, but I had to."

The hope I had been trying to fan into flame suddenly fizzled. Henry had made his decision, just as I had mine. He and I were now as diametrically opposed as the Sons of Thunder and Joshua ben-David. There was no in-between. The lines had been drawn long ago, but it was not until today that Henry and I chose sides. In that moment, I knew that nothing would ever be the same—for me or for him.

Out of the corner of a watery eye, I saw Linda's wicked, misshapen smile.

Chapter 20: The Voice of God

I walked past the first subdermal station, then the next. They were both busy. The third one had no one in line, and the women at the registration table looked at me expectantly. I walked past that one, too.

I walked in no particular direction—I just wanted to get away from the hotel, to think. I shoved my hands into my pockets to avoid the stares of disfigured people on the street. It did no good. I was not marked as they were. Suddenly part of a disfavored minority, I quickened my pace and tried hard to ignore the pointed fingers and whispered comments.

Eventually, a crowd blocked my path. I was less than thirty yards from Joshua ben-David's palace. Two familiar voices echoed over those assembled. The Sons of Thunder were prophesying again.

Half a dozen charred bodies lay scattered around the palace courtyard. The opposition was evidently getting bolder following ben-David's declaration of war, but James and John acted as though nothing were awry as they pleaded with and screamed at the people and the automatic cameras that had been set up to let the world know what terrible curse these men would call forth next.

James talked about God's mercy, and even now, if anyone would repent and follow the Messiah, who was Yeshua of Nazareth, God would forgive and receive him.

John warned against making a covenant with the wicked king. For all who did, the misery of boils and the curse of blood for water were but the first of many judgments of God on sin in these last of the last days.

I watched and listened with a different attitude than I had had in my past encounters with these men. Then I was ignorant and hardhearted. Now I knew what they said was true. Every word of it. How could I have been so blind? It was so obvious. The battle of the ages—the power and love of an Almighty God against the trickery and usurping power of Evil personified—was now reaching its fatal climactic moments. And here I was, living right in the midst of it all.

My feet carried me forward through the crowd. Disfigured faces stared in shock as they backed away, acting as though I were a leper.

James saw me first. He pointed at me and said, "Look! A child of God, redeemed from the curse."

John stopped preaching and turned. Upon making eye contact with me, he whooped loudly and leaped into the air. Both men ran toward me, and the people closest to us tripped and stumbled and fell over themselves in their haste to give us a wide berth.

The Sons of Thunder fell upon me with joyous hugs and laughing. I laughed, too, unsure of how they could possibly know anything about what had happened in the hotel suite.

"When I saw you, Thomas Beckett," James said as we walked along the narrow street, "the Holy Spirit of God spoke to me. He said, 'That one is My servant.'"

"Did you _hear_ a voice?"

"No. God speaks to our spirits, not our ears."

"That sounds like what I experienced in the hotel suite. It was a voice, not audible, but a voice just the same."

"And what did the voice say?" John said.

"It told me that as a Christian, I am now at odds with Joshua ben-David, that he is my enemy just as much as he is Jesus Christ's."

"Do you understand what it is to be a Christian?" James said.

"It means that I have identified myself with Jesus Christ— Yeshua the Messiah as you call Him."

The two men nodded. "Yes," James said, "but it goes far beyond that. You have entered into a covenant with Yeshua, a covenant instituted two thousand years ago with His blood sacrifice just outside these city walls. Just as you see those who cut a covenant with the wicked king have been physically marked, so you have been spiritually marked by your covenant with the Messiah. We have a better covenant than they, because it was sealed not by our blood but by the blood of the Lamb of God."

We walked on in silence as I let that sink in. I was in covenant with the one true God. According to my research on covenants, the participants have an attitude of total affiliation. Whatever belongs to one party is considered to belong to the other. That meant that everything that was Jesus Christ's was mine—all the power, love, wisdom, and forgiveness, there for the asking.

"I have one question," I said. James and John stopped walking and turned to face me. "The voice—the Holy Spirit—called me a 'little Christ.' What exactly does that mean?"

John folded his arms across his chest and furrowed his brow. "Christ and Messiah mean the same thing—'Anointed One.' I do not think Americans are familiar with the practice of anointing." I shook my head.

"Anointing is a commissioning for a mission, with all the power and authority needed for that mission. Moses's brother Aaron was anointed to be priest over God's people. Samuel the prophet anointed David king over Israel while Saul was still ruling. Yeshua of Nazareth was anointed by God 'to bind up the brokenhearted, to proclaim liberty to the captives, and the opening of the prison to them that are bound' as Isaiah tells us. Now that you, Thomas Beckett, have accepted Yeshua as Messiah, His anointing rests on you. As He was in this world, so are you."

"But Jesus was perfect. I am not Jesus, I can't—"

"You can do nothing. But the Spirit of God has anointed you with His power. You must not try to do things on your own. Let Messiah Yeshua work through you."

We talked for a while longer. They told me more about the Messiah and how to hear Him and respond to Him. They also spoke of the small bands of Christians all over the globe who were even now being persecuted for their faith. I was appalled at some of their tales of torture— barbaric actions perpetrated on good people simply because they refused to deny their Messiah and accept King Joshua's civic religion.

They also told me about the thousands of Jews who fled the city following ben-David's reappearance. They had gone to a place called Petra to hide in the caves there. James and John said that they would be safer there than anywhere else—that even though ben-David tried to annihilate them, he would be unable. Many of them would become martyrs, but in the end, Yeshua would return and give them the victory.

They said that I would have to join this band of refugee believers at Petra. Now that I carried the Messiah's anointing, I could no longer stay in Jerusalem, nor in any other city on earth. Joshua ben-David had seized complete control and was waging war on any and every one who refused to accept him as God.

I objected that I had not heard anything about this war through the news services. They assured me that the IDF was even now conducting covert operations directed at the destruction of the believers at Petra.

"You must remember," John said, "to a man like ben-David, image is everything. He will not allow information to reach the public if it makes him look bad. He is trying to convince us he is God."

James said, "He is a very dangerous man, Thomas Beckett. You must leave. If you will not believe us, then believe the words of Messiah Yeshua: 'When ye therefore shall see the abomination of desolation, spoken of by Daniel the prophet, stand in the holy place . . . Then let them which be in Judaea flee into the mountains.'"

"He said that?"

"Yes, Thomas Beckett, He said that."

I bade the Sons of Thunder farewell and headed toward the hotel. People in the narrow streets, hideously deformed, stared and pointed. Some shouted curses at me for associating with the two prophets. I stared at the ground to avoid their eyes.

A blur leapt out from a shadowed alleyway. Before I could react, my face had hit the cobblestones. I struggled to stand. There were two of them, each one larger than I.

I swung my right arm around, hard. It connected with a face, and two or three boils splattered sticky fluid. I heard a grunt and that attacker rolled off.

I twisted to the right and pulled myself to my knees. One man lay on the ground beside me. The other held my collar and began pummelling my rib cage with his free hand.

This was no time to be polite. I twisted left, blocking his next punch with my left arm. With the palm of my right hand, I delivered a male-specific blow that could have felled an elephant. The man howled, doubled over, and fell on his side.

I ran. Every breath was a struggle. I assumed at least two ribs were cracked. I ran anyway.

I realized I had been stupid. I had let myself be seen in public with James and John. Everyone who wanted to get his hands on them but was afraid now saw me as a potential target.

Lord Jesus, I prayed, I know now I must leave the city. Please protect me and guide me to safety.

The same feeling of warmth I had felt in the hotel room covered me again.

Breathing became easier. I ran faster.

Chapter 21: Departure

Before I could leave Jerusalem, I had some unfinished business to attend to. I ran the entire distance to the hotel and bounded up the stairs to the fourth floor. My hands still shook from adrenaline overload as I opened the door to the suite.

I was greeted by the acrid smell of something burning. Henry stood over the stove in the small kitchen, adjusting some type of apparatus situated over a boiling pot. He turned slightly when I entered but said nothing. His skin condition had become as bad as Linda's. His white shirt was stuck to his back by wet patches of broken boils.

"What is that smell?"

"Blood."

I walked over to get a closer look at Henry's invention. A frame constructed of wire hangers supported a dome of waxed paper panels over a boiling pot. Steam condensed on the paper and dripped into smaller pans strategically placed around the edge of the dome. The pot held boiling blood, but the condensation appeared to be pure water.

"Only way to get water now," Henry mumbled. "You know, this wouldn't be happening if it weren't for those two wackos out there. They say stuff, and it happens. Wish someone would just take them out."

Would you want someone to take me out, too, old friend? "You have seen what happens to anyone who attacks them."

"Yeah, but they've been doin' it wrong. We could rush them—ten or twelve guys. No way they could fire up that many people at once. Someone would get through. And that would be that. No more curses from whatever their god is. We could live in peace."

I shuddered. Henry could have easily been one of the men who attacked me, had he been with them in the shadows. His attitude was the same as theirs. The only factors that kept him from attacking me now were timing and location. If he found out with whom I had been talking . . .

Henry was right where ben-David wanted him. Whether he had been brainwashed or was merely following the path of his own choices, I could not say. Maybe my perspective was the one that had changed. I was the one who was swimming against the current—Henry was going the same direction as everyone else.

The phone rang. I was closer, so I answered.

"Hello, Mr. Beckett," said a man's voice.

"Yes, who is this?"

"I serve King Joshua ben-David. According to our records, you have not visited one of the subdermal stations yet. That is not good, Mr. Beckett."

"What is this about? What is your name?"

"We saw you talking to the blasphemers today. You should choose your friends more carefully. They are lying to you. Do nothing foolish, Mr. Beckett. Your life depends on it. We are watching." Click.

I replaced the handset.

"Who was that?" Henry said.

"He didn't say."

I turned over the options once more in my mind. One thing was clear. I could stay here no longer, not even in my own hotel suite. I could not even trust the man who had been my best friend for years. I would collect a few essentials and then work on obtaining transportation to Petra.

"Where's yours?" Henry said.

"I beg you pardon?"

"Your subdermal, pretty boy—where is it?"

I shoved my hands into my pockets and walked into the living area. Caught.

"You don't have it. Oh, you've messed up now, Beckett."

I turned. Henry never called me Beckett. "What do you mean?"

"Haven't you heard? The deadline for subdermals is midnight tonight. After that, ben-David's soldiers start arresting people."

"Midnight? That's too soon."

"Too soon? You could go now and be back in time for dinner. It's not too soon for anyone who wants to obey the law." Henry approached me and grabbed my arms with two misshapen hands.

I saw in his eyes an emotion I had never seen before. Hatred.

His voice was low and menacing. "I did this thing. And I got the boils to prove it. You have to do it, too. Everyone in the world does. You're no different from anyone else. I know you want to run—I can see it in your eyes. But you can't get away. You can't hide from the king. If you run, he will find you, and when he does . . . I'm gonna ask him if I can have the honor of personally breaking your neck."

I left the hotel empty-handed, without checking out or saying goodbye to anyone. I walked for miles. Three cabs and a bus had already traded their debit card readers for the new subdermal readers. I was effectively broke.

The dull, diffused sunlight fighting its way through the debris of Black Knight gave way to the fuzzy, blood-red light of the moon. I was now well outside the Old City, and I hoped no one lurked in the darkness who had seen me earlier with James and John. I kept my hands hidden and my eyes open.

The air was filled with the soft moans of those afflicted with the boils, which by now was nearly everyone in Jerusalem. They were all my enemies by way of covenant, but instead of fear, I felt a deep compassion for them.

Henry was at least partly right—we were no different. The only thing that separated us was our decision whom to trust. They were just as human as I, and a covenant with Messiah Yeshua was just as available to them as it was to me. But they would never experience the joy and peace I had found. They had made their decision. They had cut their covenant.

My thoughts turned to the immediate problem of transportation to Petra. I had given up on trying to find a rental car agency—they would probably report me to whoever was on the other end of that menacing phone conversation. I needed something fast and durable enough for the desert.

I heard a disturbance ahead of me. Several people were breaking into a store. The owner was not happy. An IDF Land Rover drove past me and stopped in front of the store. The would-be robbers scattered, and four soldiers tumbled out of the vehicle, hitting the ground in a dead run.

I would have little time. I hopped into the driver's seat and floored the accelerator. All four doors slammed shut as I sped into the night.

I knew that the main roads would be patrolled, and a renegade IDF vehicle ignoring checkpoints and speed limits would be a little too obvious. Two kilometers outside the city limits, I turned off the Land Rover's headlamps and left the road in favor of the open desert. Driving across wilderness terrain with only the faint ruby glow of the moon for light would make for a long and slow journey, but I found that prospect infinitely preferable to being caught.

I pointed the nose of the vehicle in a direction I hoped was east, praying constantly for God to lead me to the cliffs of Petra. The basic route would not be difficult: east to the Jordan River; after finding a shallow area and fording the river, I would travel south to the Dead Sea; from there I hoped to be able to locate Petra. Navigating at night with no stars visible was something sailors learned to do thousands of years ago, but I am no sailor. Without the Big Dipper and the North Star, I am lost.

At the end of about two hours of rough, off road driving made more difficult by the need to avoid any people, lights, or vehicles, I had crossed the Jordan. My nerves were frazzled and the Land Rover's fuel tank was nearly empty.

I had convinced myself that I would soon be walking when I saw a cluster of angular shadows against the dim horizon to my left. It might have been an IDF outpost, but it was more likely an Arab or Russian camp left over from Ezekiel's War. Many such camps still had fuel and supplies and decomposed bodies of soldiers, all just waiting to be plundered. It was not so much that the Israelis were lax in cleaning up after the war, but more that the task was so monumental.

I parked the Land Rover out of sight behind a small berm, and grabbing the rifle, I walked toward the camp. I could discern voices emanating from behind the tents. They were shouting. I ran behind one of the tents and listened. The two male voices spoke Hebrew. They argued as a third voice, that of a woman, sobbed quietly.

One of the men issued a sharp order that ended all other discussion. Peering around the corner of the tent, I saw two soldiers, part of Joshua ben-David's private guard, drag an Israeli man and woman to their feet in the beams of the vehicle's headlights. The man was wearing brown pants and an open collared shirt, and the woman wore a long pale blue dress. Since neither was dressed for a desert excursion, I assumed they were part of the group of Israelis that fled Jerusalem the night the resurrected Joshua ben-David made his appearance at the Temple.

The soldiers stood their bound and gagged prisoners side-by-side and stepped away into the shadows. Before I realized what was happening, two gunshots rang out. I jumped. The man and woman spasmed and crumpled to the ground, a bullet through each heart.

The soldiers got into their vehicle and left. I ran to the fallen bodies to see if there was anything I could do. They were both dead.

I was stunned by the execution-style killings. Those had been Israeli soldiers in the service of a man they believed was the Messiah, yet they had acted more like Hitler's Nazis than anything else. If the argument I overheard had been any indication, the junior officer did not wish to kill these fellow Israelis. In the end, though, he was just following orders.

I stood and turned to survey the camp. Several AK-47 rifles lay near battle-clad skeletons. The four armored personnel carriers parked around the tents were of Russian design, but the two dozen uniforms labelled the bones as Syrian. Their remains lay scattered about in positions consistent with the rest of that bizarre battle. They had apparently all turned on each other in a moment and died at the hands of their own countrymen.

I stepped over two of the bodies to get to the first vehicle. The personnel carriers were fueled by diesel, but most military units used gasoline powered generators to fulfill their electrical needs while camped. I opened the lid of a fuel can mounted to the back of the personnel carrier and sniffed its contents. Diesel.

There was a second can, this one with a yellow painted lid, mounted on the other side of the door. I walked around the remains of a soldier who had been killed trying to flee to the relative safety of the armored vehicle, and I opened the other can. That one held gasoline.

I freed that can and one other yellow topped can from their mountings and walked back to the Land Rover. I found a long funnel in the back—evidently ben-David's troops were no strangers to this method of refueling—and filled the tank.

I oriented myself with the Jordan, sent up a brief prayer, and was on my way.

The Land Rover's fuel tank was approaching empty again by the time morning light began showing itself as a rambling blue-black florescence surrounding the obscure crimson moon. I was relieved to see mountains in the distance, but with the approaching light, the easily visible IDF vehicle would be a handicap. I hid it as best I could and began gathering supplies for my trek.

The soldiers were kind enough to have left me two canteens of water and a small bag of dates. I attached both canteens to one belt and strapped it around my waist. I placed the dates in a pocket along with two clips of ammunition to go with the Israeli assault rifle stored behind the front seat.

I had no doubt that I looked comical. Dirty, charcoal gray slacks and a white shirt, ripped and bloodied from the attack by the two Israelis, were complemented by the green belt and two canteens. I carried a rifle and was badly in need of a shave.

North America, would you trust this man to bring you the news? I chuckled and ran a hand through my dirty, ragged hair as I tried to decide if there was anything else I might need—besides a bath.

I picked up the charcoal gray sport coat that lay on the

passenger's seat. One never knows what one might need in the desert. I laid it down. The desert is hot. Who needs a coat? I picked it back up. Better to have it and not need it than to suffer from want.

Before I could change my mind again, I took my first steps toward the mountains on the horizon.

I did not walk in a straight line. As much as possible, I wanted to be near rocks, bushes, or some other type of cover in order to have a place to hide when the inevitable IDF helicopter flew overhead. Whether or not they cared about capturing me, they would at least want their Land Rover back.

I had been walking for about two hours when I heard the distinctive whup-whup-whup of a helicopter approaching. I ducked under the branches of the largest bush I could see and draped my suit coat over me to hide the white shirt. The helicopter passed without changing direction or speed, and I resumed my journey.

My heart skipped half a beat with the thought that the suit coat I had almost left with the Land Rover might have just saved me from detection.

I kept walking until I could no longer feel my legs beneath me. I tried to be as sparing with my water consumption as my body would allow, but the fierce desert heat drained sweat from me, and I drained water from the canteens. Part of me marvelled that the sun could be so hot yet appear so dim.

When I heard the second helicopter I was near another abandoned military camp. I must have been dazed by dehydration, because I did not hear it until it was almost on top of me. I stumbled into one of the tents. It was hotter in the tent than it was outside. There was no breeze, only the persistent stench of death.

The helicopter landed inside the camp, and I could hear voices over the sound of the rotors. They had seen me. As I peered through the tent door, my knees buckled under me. A dozen soldiers ran toward my tent.

I had to fight. There were too many of them, but I at least had to try. I raised the rifle to my shoulder with quivering arms. The barrel swayed in odd circles. My vision tunnelled. The soldiers were much closer, but they blurred as the borders of my eyesight closed in on them. Would I hit anything when I pulled the trigger? I squeezed.

That small effort was more than my body was capable of in its exhausted state. My arms dropped, and the rifle fell to the ground. I thought ironically, <u>Maybe I will surrender, after all</u>.

I remember hearing gunshots as my face met the sand and the world darkened around me.

Voices filtered through the darkness. Strange voices. I could not understand what they were saying. My eyes stubbornly refused to open. I groaned in protest. That got the attention of the voices.

"So, the brave soldier awakes?" A man's voice.

<u>Soldiers. They have come to capture me. I have to fight</u>. I tried sitting. A hand on my shoulder pushed me back onto the flat, hard surface.

"Be still. You don't want to pull out the IV," said a woman's voice.

"IV?" I managed to croak.

"Yes. You were severely dehydrated, almost dead. You should be glad we found you."

"I think he will be all right, now," said the man's voice.

I tried opening my eyes again. This time, they cooperated. I was in a vehicle, looking up at the face of a Bedouin, judging from the way he was dressed.

"You have been through quite a lot, my friend."

"You could say that."

"Don't be afraid. You will be safe with us."

"Thank you."

Pause. "I was just noticing that you have no boils," he said.

"No."

"So you have not received the mark of ben-David. You have no subdermal debit card?"

"It looks as though you have not, either."

He shrugged. "In the desert we have little need for the economy or religion of Joshua Cohen."

Joshua <u>Cohen</u>? Clearly, this man was no devotee of the current civic religion. I grunted. Perhaps it was time to take a risk.

"Neither have I."

"So tell me, if you do not subscribe to the king's religion, of whose faith are you?"

I swallowed. I was in the middle of a very dangerous game. This man who held my life in his hands now wanted a confession of what I believed. It was a game of trust—a tug of war to see if the truth would make us enemies or friends. If this Bedouin was no fan of the king, he might be a follower of Messiah Yeshua—or he might be a spy sent by the king to ferret out the Messiah's followers. But if that were so, why would I still be alive?

"I . . . ."

"Come, now. It must be a strong faith. We have heard what the king plans to do to any who refuse to accept him as God."

"I am a Christian. I serve Jesus the Messiah." There. I had said it.

"Oh, that is foolish, my friend. You could lose everything, even your life, by professing a belief in a god other than the mighty Joshua ben-David. If you are caught rebelling against the royal decree, things would go very badly for you. Assuming, of course, you are running from the king's men."

"Joshua Cohen is no god."

"But he was raised from the dead. He has brought peace to our world. He wields miraculous powers. Even his image speaks and moves as if alive."

I struggled to prop myself up on my elbows. The vehicle was no longer at the military camp, but it was not moving, either. I was at a disadvantage, not knowing where we were. One thing was certain. I was committed to my course of action.

I squinted against the swimming sensations in my head and continued. "King Joshua looks good. He is flashy and impressive, and I do not know how he does many of the things I have seen him do, but I am convinced that he is not who he claims to be. He is certainly not God." The man exchanged a look with the older of two women that lasted several seconds. He then pulled off his turban, revealing a shining olive-colored scalp that was winning the war against a retreating hairline. He smiled and extended a hand in greeting. "Welcome to the family of God."

That was no Bedouin. That was Habib. He and his wife and daughter were out on one of the frequent scavenging missions necessary to obtain supplies for the exiles at Petra. They brought me back with them, and I was welcomed by the inhabitants of Petra as a member of their large family.

That brings us to the present, here in the caves of Petra.

I am not sure what I expected of this place as I wandered through the desert, but it was not the combination refugee camp, fortress, guerilla base, church, multicultural museum that I found.

Not everyone understands each other's language, but in the past few weeks, I have seen more genuine love than I have at any one time in my life. If a need is expressed, it is immediately filled, often from an unexpected source. God speaks to these people, and they respond.

As I glance back over the pages I have written, I am amazed that God's patience and love have brought me this far. I still have much to learn about the Messiah, and I have a feeling there will be plenty of work for me to do here before He returns to establish His reign on the earth.

So even though my story is finished for now, the writer in me will not allow my hand to stop moving. There may be no valid reason for me to do so, but I will continue to record events as they transpire in the hope that my musings will encourage you to carry on in your faith.

Chapter 22: Petra

During the past few weeks, I have been learning more about Yeshua of Nazareth and about God's ultimate plan to bring peace to our troubled world. Rabbi Aaron Dyan, who was instrumental in discovering the long lost Ark of the Covenant nearly four years ago, is our resident celebrity. He also serves as a sort of spiritual leader, and he has been tutoring me.

I made the mistake one day of calling him a Christian. He informed me rather forcefully that he was still a Jew, but he was a "completed Jew" now that he had found his Messiah. He uses the books of the New Testament as well as the Old in his teaching, proudly proclaiming that God's entire Word was recorded by Jews.

He is even more proud of James and John, the Sons of Thunder. Their mission was one of the first things he showed me from Scripture.

Rabbi Dyan emerged through the low entrance to the back portion of the cave into the main room where I and four others sat on woven mats on the floor. The one woman in the room sat behind the semicircle of men in what I felt was a bizarre tip of the hat to Middle Eastern tradition.

It was time for class. This was my first session since arriving at Petra, and despite myself, I was a little nervous. The others in the room were old timers, having sat under Rabbi Dyan's instruction for as long as two months. The rabbi was in charge of introducing the new arrivals at Petra to their new faith and preparing them for the imminent return of the Messiah.

Rabbi Dyan sat on a mat before the class, opened a large Bible, and said simply, "Revelation chapter 11." There was a rustling of paper as we opened the books in front of us to that place. The rabbi began reading with the third verse.

> And I will give power unto my two witnesses, and they shall prophesy a thousand two hundred and threescore days, clothed in sackcloth . . . And if any man will hurt them, fire proceedeth out of their mouth, and devoureth their enemies . . . These have power to shut heaven, that it rain not in the days of their prophecy: and have power over waters to turn them to blood, and to smite the earth with all plagues, as often as they will.

"James and John are these two witnesses," he said. "All that is prophesied of them must come to pass." The rabbi continued for several verses. I relate here only the ones that hit me the hardest:

> And when they shall have finished their testimony, the beast that ascendeth out of the bottomless pit shall make war against them, and shall overcome them, and kill them. And their dead bodies shall lie in the street of the great city . . . nations shall see their dead bodies three days and an half, and shall not suffer their dead bodies to be put in graves . . . And after three days and an half the Spirit of life from God entered into them, and they stood upon their feet; and great fear fell upon them which saw them. And they heard a great voice from heaven saying unto them, Come up hither. And they ascended up to heaven in a cloud; and their enemies beheld them.

Rabbi Dyan closed the book and paused. "When you see the two witnesses lying in the streets of Jerusalem, look up, for Messiah returns soon."

James and John, the invincible Sons of Thunder, lying dead in the streets of Jerusalem? It was unthinkable, yet this ancient book spoke specifically about their ministry. That passage, more than anything else, erased any trace of doubt there may have been in my mind regarding the choice I made to follow Jesus. He would return very soon, and I would be ready to greet Him.

Suddenly, sitting on that mat in Rabbi Dyan's cave, my entire focus changed. I realized that I had lived my whole life on survival mode. Even my decision to follow the Messiah had been based at least partly in my desire not to subject myself to the punishment I saw the rest of the world enduring.

Survival mode was rendered moot at that moment. As the Sons of Thunder said, I now carried the anointing of Yeshua of Nazareth. The awesome responsibility of that anointing began to sink in. I had a mission in the same way James and John had a mission. The only difference was that mine had not been written in a book two thousand years ago.

In fact, at that moment I had no idea what my mission would be.

Habib found me the next day by the water basin, a large hole in the rock where water had been stored prior to James and John's proclamation of no rain. He was wearing the same Bedouin robes he had worn on the day he and his family rescued me. The turban was gone, though, and his sweating scalp glistened in the dim light.

Habib said, "Thomas Beckett, I have a mission for you."

"Oh?"

"Come to my home. I want you to meet someone."

I was unaware that my mental question had been perceived as a prayer, but here was the answer.

Habib's home was larger than most of the dwellings I had seen since my arrival. He explained that space at Petra was divided on a first come, first served basis. When he and his family arrived, there were fewer than one hundred people here—consequently, they have more space than the average family.

He told me of the ten single Israeli men who helped them establish the civilization at Petra. "They were such organizers," he said, and his enthusiasm allowed several small pieces of date to escape his mouth. He continued without noticing. "I tell you, Mr. Beckett, the hand of God was on those men. They knew exactly where to find the supplies we needed. They knew how to avoid Joshua Cohen's men—yes, even then the king was after us secretly, covertly. And if one of us ever became sick or hurt—" he threw his hands into the air in an expansive gesture "—all they had to do was say the word, and the person was healed instantly."

"That sounds like someone I know."

"You knew one of these men?"

"No, but I had an encounter with a young Israeli preacher in New York who sounds just like the men you describe. I saw him raise a woman from the dead."

Habib paused and his eyes reddened. His wife looked at him and smiled. He said, "Do you remember my daughter, Miri?"

"Of course," I said, recalling the strong, steady teenage hands that had cared for my medical needs in the desert. "She was with you when you rescued me."

"She would not be with us today had it not been for those men. None of us would be."

"So what happened to them? Where did they go?"

"You no doubt remember the Great Disappearance?" he said, regaining his enthusiasm. "It was like that. It was a small disappearance. One moment they were here, and the next they were gone. We were not surprised, though. They told us it would be that way. Still, it was a loss."

I told Habib about my research in New York and how much bigger their disappearance was than he imagined. My best guess was that there had been over one hundred thousand of these Israelis running around performing miracles and preaching about Messiah Yeshua.

"There were one-hundred forty-four thousand of them, Mr. Beckett."

"I thought you only knew of the ten here."

Habib walked to the side of the room and picked up a black book. "This tells us of one-hundred forty-four thousand, Mr. Beckett. Twelve thousand from each of the twelve tribes of Israel."

I should have known the Bible would have something to say about such a remarkable group. Habib showed me the passages relating to these men, and his wife brought us some herbal tea and more dates.

When we had finished our impromptu Bible study, I said, "You were saying something about a mission for me?"

"Yes. Sam should be here any minute. He will tell you of your mission." Habib's mischievous grin heightened my anticipation. Whatever this assignment was, Habib obviously felt it would be a custom fit for me.

The doorway darkened a few moments later and Habib's wife pulled the goat skin curtain aside to reveal a tall, lanky man with an unruly tuft of red hair and ubiquitous freckles.

"My friend, Mr. Isaacs. Welcome. Meet my new friend, Thomas Beckett. Mr. Beckett, meet Sam Isaacs."

We shook hands, and Sam smiled just long enough to be polite before lapsing into the same impassive expression he had when he walked in. My first impression was that this was a man unaccustomed to dealing with real people. I had seen the same face, the same slightly stooped shoulders, on dozens of computer techies. If Sam Isaacs did not know a megabyte from a modem, I would eat my shirt.

Perceiving that Sam had no intention of carrying the conversation, Habib jumped in. "Sam is our resident guide to the World Wide Web. He has walked where cyberspace angels fear to tread." Sam's face flushed and Habib laughed.

"Are you telling me you have computers here at Petra?"

"But of course, Mr. Beckett. We are not savages. Petra may not have all the comforts of home, but it does have all the necessities. Isn't that so, Mr. Isaacs?"

Sam said, "Yes, well, I guess God knew that I would be lost if I couldn't go online."

"No, Mr. Isaacs, we would be lost. My friend Sam is too modest, Mr. Beckett. He doesn't understand that the information he gleans for us from the Web is a lifeline of encouragement. With his skills, we have been able to keep in touch with other believers across the globe. That is very important in times such as these."

"So what is the assignment?"

"Mr. Isaacs?"

The tall man twitched slightly as if having to adjust to a bright light after being in a darkened room. Then he said, "Habib and I want you to go online with us and tell people what you know about Joshua ben-David and about James and John."

"You see, Mr. Beckett, we followers of Yeshua have a responsibility to spread the word of His kingdom. Even now, when the darkness seems greatest—or perhaps because the darkness is great—we must testify to the world that Yeshua of Nazareth is the Messiah."

"What good will that do for those who have accepted the king's mark?" I willed myself not to think about Henry and Linda and steeled myself for the answer I already knew.

Habib shrugged. "It will do them no good. They have made their decision. We testify of the Messiah as an act of war against the enemies of God, so that on the Day of Judgment, they will have no excuse. As the Word says, 'And they overcame him by the blood of the Lamb, and by the word of their testimony; and they loved not their lives unto the death.' Every one of us is ready to die for the sake of spreading the word of the Messiah's coming. Besides, there may still be a few people who have not bowed their knee to Joshua Cohen. We may be able to bring even more people into the kingdom of God. The Web will be our vehicle for reaching those people. Either way, we must do what we can."

Habib was right. With every gift comes a certain responsibility, and we had been given the gift of eternal life. We had an eternal responsibility to serve our Savior in whatever way we could.

I had to admit that the idea of using me as the vehicle for a multi-media message to the world was a good one. People could ignore a lesser known face and voice, but I had earned the respect and attention of millions of viewers worldwide.

"All right," I said, "what do you want me to do?"

The plan was fairly simple. Sam Isaacs was a "stealth hack" who could crack any encryption code in the business, and who knew

137

techniques for hiding his trail on the Web so no one would be able to track our location.

We would make video clips of me exposing the truth about Joshua Cohen, explaining the significance of the subdermals, and supporting the message of the Sons of Thunder. Sam would then feed these messages onto the Web in what he termed a "broadcast linkup." In short, every house in the world that had a computer or a television set would receive the video, whether they wanted to or not. We would interrupt newscasts, press conferences, online chat rooms, sitcoms, and soap operas. Citizens of earth would find their virtual mailboxes full of multimedia messages about the Messiah.

I have to admit that the implementation of this plan was fun. I wrote my own copy and delivered it in an intimate conversational style, seated on the edge of a large rock—sometimes walking—and gesturing as needed to emphasize my point. It was good to be in front of a camera again, even if the sparse video equipment available was not the high-tech gear I was accustomed to.

We really did not need top end video equipment, though. By the time Sam Isaacs had finished enhancing and editing the clips, we had a funky, hard-hitting collection of pop culture sound bites that no one would be able to ignore.

Twenty-seven hours after I had finished my part, Sam clicked the "Send" button and initiated the first broadcast of "The Whole Truth."

Chapter 23: The Trap

For every attack, there is a counter attack until the final battle is fought that determines who wins the war. "The Whole Truth" was our opening salvo in a war against King Joshua that was begun by one hundred forty-four thousand young Israeli bachelors nearly four years ago. The king's counter attack was swift, arriving a short two days after our initial broadcast.

I was attending Rabbi Dyan's worship service in the amphitheater constructed by the Romans when they occupied Petra. It has since been cleaned and refurbished by the current inhabitants, and serves as our central meeting place. Sam Isaacs quietly, albeit clumsily, approached and sat next to me, so obviously wanting not to interrupt the service that he actually created more of a disturbance than if he had crossed directly in front of the rabbi.

"Hello, Sam. What is it?"

"There's something you should see."

I stared at the screen in disbelief, but there was no denying that the faces on the monitor were those of Anthony Ian Beckett and his mother, Carolyn.

"Please . . . play it again," I whispered. The image flickered and the message began anew.

Carolyn said, "Hello, Thomas, it's me. Surprised? Listen, I know we haven't been getting along at all since the divorce, but when I started seeing your messages all over TV and on the computer at home, I realized just how much I missed you. So Tony and I flew right over. That's when they told us you were gone."

"Look, Pop," Anthony said, "I'm really sorry about how we left everything. We should talk. Why don't you come see us?"

"We're staying at the hotel, next door to your old buddy Henry's room. Take care. We'll see you soon."

The image of Carolyn and Anthony smiling froze on the screen. Sam said, "Mr. Beckett, I'm sorry. I don't know how they were able to find us. For all I can tell, this might just be a broadcast message like what we have been sending. Maybe everyone in the Middle East has it." That was more than Sam Isaacs had said to me since I met him. He must have seen the anguish on my face and was trying to make this whole thing easier on me.

Habib, who had walked in at some point unannounced, said, "It is a trap, Thomas."

Of course it was a trap. I was sure King Joshua's desire to lure me out into the open was second only to his desire to destroy the Sons of Thunder. He was obviously using my family as bait. Carolyn did not have the kind of finances to be able to hop on a flight to Israel on a moment's notice. And I even doubted her sincerity in saying she missed me.

Still, a deep compassion for them overwhelmed me. I knew God loved them, and despite all our bad history, they were my family. With my new view of life from behind the cross of Jesus, I realized that I loved them, too.

Even if it was a trap, my desire was to rescue them from ben-David's rule. Neither Carolyn nor Anthony seemed to be afflicted with the sores that everyone with a subdermal was getting. That fact alone gave me hope. Apparently, pressure to covenant with ben-David was not as strong overseas as it was in Israel, but I knew the pressure would mount and eventually both of them would succumb.

If Carolyn and Anthony had not taken their subdermals yet, then there was still hope that they could be persuaded to covenant with the Messiah instead. Any rescue attempt would be risky, but it would be worth the chance to see my ex-wife and son enter the kingdom of God with me.

"Habib," I said, "I know it is a trap."

"But you wish to go see them, anyway. Perhaps to save them from the king?" Their lack of skin disease had not been lost to Habib. "Thomas, my friend, I can see it in your eyes, but the risks would be too great. I cannot allow an expedition of this kind. We would be going into the very heart of the enemy's camp. How could we come out alive?"

I nodded. "I cannot ask you to walk into a trap with me or to send any of your people. But this is something I must do. These people are my family, my responsibility. As long as there is still a chance they could be saved, I must do what I can. The rest is up to God. You told me that with the anointing of Jesus comes great responsibility. This is it for me. This is my area of responsibility, and if I die in the attempt—well, I guess I will see you on the other side."

Habib stared at the ground momentarily before meeting my eyes again. "I suppose I knew it would be this way. Come. We have much planning to do."

Jerusalem was too heavily patrolled at night for any reasonable chance of success, and Habib argued that Joshua Cohen's men would be expecting us to come at night. We decided to find a way to get into the city in full daylight without arousing suspicion. We could get near Jerusalem in one of the plundered vehicles from the war, but we would have to hide it before we reached civilization.

Then there was the question of our appearance. I suggested that since we would be walking into the city, we should dress as Bedouins. It seemed to work well for Habib and his recon teams. That suggestion gained a hearty laugh from all assembled. Bedouins never venture into the cities any more, a peaceful protest to the governance of the king who subdued the Arabs. If the authorities thought we were Bedouins, we would be arrested miles from the hotel.

"No," Habib said, "we must appear as residents of Jerusalem. That means we must have boils, or we will be suspect in their eyes. Now it occurs to me that the gel carried by many soldiers as a burn remedy could be formed to look like boils. We have a good supply of it here. But the gel is clear and would need to be painted in order to look realistic." He paused. We waited. "I happen to know someone here at Petra who may be able to help us with that."

That someone was Habib's daughter, Miri.

As she painted my boils, she told me her story. First, her name was Miriam, but she hated it and would not allow anyone to call her by it. It was an old woman's name. "Miri" sounded unique and strong and feminine all at once, and she liked that. Studying her clean, youthful appearance and the fire behind her eyes, I decided the name fit.

Miri was not a teen as I had first assumed. She was twenty-five and an accomplished artist who worked for an advertising agency in Tel Aviv until the day her mother had called and invited her over for dinner.

Habib had accepted Yeshua as Messiah just days after the culmination of Ezekiel's War and had spent the following two months persuading his wife to accept the new faith. In a divinely ordained event, one of the young Israeli miracle workers came to Habib's house that evening mere minutes before Miri arrived.

When she entered the house, she was literally assaulted with the good news of Yeshua the Messiah. Every time the exuberant Israeli paused for a breath, Habib would jump in. After half an hour of this barrage, Miri, who by her own admission was a stubborn child who rarely did anything her father wanted her to, sat at the dining table and said, "Yes, this is what I want."

141

No sooner had Miri made a confession of her faith in Yeshua of Nazareth, the Israeli preacher lifted his hands to the sky and said, "Abba, these three should be baptized according to Your will."

Suddenly, the four people found themselves not in Habib's house, but outside, surrounded by trees. Beyond the trees to her left, Miri heard the gentle rush of a small waterfall. The family of three looked around in stunned disorientation.

The young Israeli smiled. "Over there," he said, pointing in the direction of the waterfall sound. "That is the Jordan River. Let us baptize you." They did not argue, but walked to the river's edge. The preacher baptized Habib first, then Patma his wife, then Miri.

As Miri came out of the water, the Israeli told the family not to return to Tel Aviv, but to go directly to Petra, by the Dead Sea. There they would be protected by God's hand in the days to come. "And if anyone stops you on the way, remember, it is written: 'No weapon that is formed against thee shall prosper; and every tongue that shall rise against thee in judgment thou shalt condemn. This is the heritage of the servants of the LORD, and their righteousness is of me, saith the LORD.'" With that, he looked heavenward and vanished.

They were not stopped along the way, and Miri remembered thinking how odd his parting words had been. Later, however, on one of the many covert missions Miri went on with her father, they were stopped by one of the IDF's clean-up crews. It was these soldiers' job to find and bury the bodies left out in the open following Israel's miraculous victory in Ezekiel's War. They tended to be greedy, generally carrying away more plunder than bodies to be buried. Consequently, they became agitated when they found Habib's family making off with supplies from one of the tents.

The soldiers lined them up at gunpoint outside, cursing them for their irreligious desecration of the ground where these brave soldiers had died. The soldiers took their places in the firing squad.

"Ready."

"No weapon formed against us will prosper," Miri whispered through her terror.

"Take aim."

"It is written," Miri screamed. "No weapon formed against thee shall prosper!"

"Fire."

Miri heard only one gunshot, magnified six times. The sound echoed across the valley.

Silence.

Miri opened one eye to see six soldiers and an officer staring open mouthed. Habib began laughing and bent down to pick up six flattened lead slugs out of the sand in front of them. He threw them at the soldiers, who left without further discussion.

Miri finished with her story at the same moment she finished with my disguise. "There," she said triumphantly. "Your own mother would not know it was you."

She handed me a small broken mirror. I was shocked at the transformation. I could have been anyone with a subdermal.

I have beheld my face in a mirror tens of thousands of times over the course of my life. I have been pleased, amused, disappointed, and in recent years even frightened by what I beheld in the looking glass. But never, <u>never</u> have I experienced violent nausea at the sight of my own image. Until that moment.

"Well?"

"Miri, I don't know whether to hug you or punch you."

She laughed. A pretty sound.

"I suppose I am ready."

"Mr. Beckett," she said as I rose from the chair. "I told you that story so you would understand—you and my father do not go to Jerusalem alone. The Holy Spirit of God goes with you, and He will protect you. Only trust Him as He speaks to your heart."

Divine protection. In the back of my mind, I think I already knew it was there—my meeting with Habib in the middle of the desert argued in favor of it—but I had never thought much about going into a dangerous situation with God as my advocate. New hope for success was born, and I smiled. "No weapon formed against thee shall prosper."

"It is written."

"Thank you, Miri." I hugged her briefly and walked to the mouth of the cave, where Habib waited for me.

"It is time," he said. "But first, let us pray for the success of our mission."

"And for your safe return," Miri said from behind me.

There at the entrance to Habib's family dwelling, we three joined hands with Habib's wife Patma and prayed for success and safety. My friend's confidence was inspiring. The hope Miri had planted in my heart began to grow into something more like faith—complete confidence that God does watch over His people and that He would watch over us this day.

Chapter 24: The Enemy Camp

"Remember," Habib said as we walked along the road, "the boils are extremely painful. To avoid suspicion, we must act as though we are in pain as well. You will know how to act by observing the people we see."

We did not see many people, and the ones we saw hid their suffering behind veils and hoods. Still, we knew the people were there from the constant moaning making its way past the walls of houses. Fighting against everything my body wanted to do, we slowed our pace and walked stooped, staring at the ground and moaning whenever we had an audience. I wanted to run, or at least to quicken our pace, to get to the hotel sooner, but that would have been a dead giveaway.

No words passed between us on the last leg of our journey. Those sharing a bond of suffering rarely talk, and when they do, it is about how they feel. That would have been no help to our mission. Except for the constant high doses of adrenaline being pumped through my bloodstream and the slight cramp between my shoulders from walking with bad posture, I felt quite well.

When we finally reached the door of the hotel, Habib's eyes locked with mine. I nodded slightly, assuring him that I remembered our story. If asked why we were at the hotel, we would say that we were visiting a sick friend. I also assured Habib with my eyes that I was ready for whatever might happen next. The following minutes would be the most dangerous part of our mission. Here, at this hotel, is where Joshua ben-David's trap would be set.

I went first through the revolving door into the posh hotel lobby. Couches stood along the walls on large, thick rugs. The lobby was the size of a basketball court, and the front desk stood at the opposite end. To the left of it were the elevators, and the restaurant was visible to the right. The infected desk clerk watched the television perched on the right end of the desk and showed no sign of acknowledging the presence of any new guests.

Habib tapped my arm, and I followed him toward the elevators. As we passed the front desk, an image from the television caught my attention. It was Henry's disfigured face. He was at ben-David's palace, with James and John in the background, shouting at King Joshua. I paused to watch over the clerk's shoulder while Habib crossed the remaining distance to the elevators and pressed the "up" button. About one hundred soldiers stood between ben-David and the Sons of Thunder.

At once I had a longing to be the face in front of the camera. This situation had the potential of escalating into a confrontation of decisive proportions, and the reporter in me wanted the scoop.

Henry was saying that King ben-David had called again for the death of these two men and the destruction of the God that they served. This, he said, was the day that would happen.

The elevator dinged just as the soldiers raised their weapons and burst into flames. Habib tugged on my sleeve but I held him in place so he would watch, too.

I could still see ben-David through the wall of fire leaping up from the charred bodies, his face impassive and arrogant. He looked like the Devil himself. James and John turned to face the mob that was on the verge of attacking. John shook his head as if to say, "Don't do it."

Too late.

As one, the crowd of civilian bystanders screamed and lunged at the two men. Henry looked over his shoulder, dropped the microphone, and ran to join them.

"No." The word escaped my mouth before I had a chance to stop it. Habib jabbed my ribs. The clerk made no indication that he heard or cared. He continued to moan softly, too intent on his own suffering to notice my outburst.

This was Henry's rush. This is what he had talked about here at the hotel when I last saw him. It would be his final rebellion against God, and I chose not to watch.

I turned to Habib. He winced, and his face reflected the red glow of new fire on the television screen. Not removing his gaze from the scene of devastation, Habib whispered, "He was your friend?"

I nodded.

"I am sorry, Thomas." A pause, then he met my eyes. "Come. The living still have work to do."

We had to wait for another elevator, and by the time it arrived, several people stood behind us, also waiting to board. I would have preferred it otherwise, but our disguises were good enough to fool nearly anyone. I avoided the temptation to turn and look at them, telling myself not to be afraid—God's protection was on us.

The elevator signalled its arrival and opened its doors. Habib and I stepped to the back and turned around. Our riding companions would be two large men in dark suits and—

I elbowed Habib's ribs and he nodded. It was Carolyn and

Anthony. The two men were ben-David's guards, ready to arrest or kill me on sight, no doubt. Judging from Carolyn and Anthony's conversation, they had just come from the restaurant.

"Floor?" said one of the men.

"Six," Habib answered.

The doors closed, and as the elevator began its ascent, I wondered how and when Habib and I would be able to subdue the guards. Surprise would be our only advantage over the larger and assumably well-trained men. I never finished my plan.

An abrupt stop. Silence. The guard closest to the control panel pressed buttons, and the other reached inside a coat pocket for his cell phone.

The lights went out, and there was the soft sound of crumpling bodies as two large bodies fell unconscious on the elevator floor. A soft glow illuminated the inside of the elevator, but it was different from the normal lights. Carolyn and Anthony regarded the fallen men, and then looked at Habib and me. I removed my hood and was denied any look of recognition from either of them.

I said, "Carolyn? Anthony? Don't you know me? I'm Thomas."

"Thomas? You look awful."

"Pop!"

My son and I embraced under Carolyn's icy stare.

If pressed, I would have to say that we were in that elevator for the better part of an hour, though it felt like only a few minutes. I told Carolyn and Anthony about my newfound faith in Jesus the Messiah, and about the new life I had found at Petra. I also told them about Joshua ben-David and the dangers of accepting his mark. I apologized to Carolyn for the divorce and to Anthony for not being there when he needed me. I asked their forgiveness, and I begged them to come back to Petra with us.

Anthony hung on every word and even became a little misty-eyed at my request for forgiveness. Carolyn looked at me with the same expression I saw on the king's face through the flames of his soldiers' bodies. Before I even asked if they would return to Petra with us, I knew that Carolyn would have no part of it. True, she had not yet cut the covenant with the anti-Messiah, but in her heart, she had a long time ago.

The elevator doors opened, and we found ourselves on the ground floor again. Habib, Anthony, and I stepped over and around the guards and out of the elevator.

"Carolyn, please," I said. "None of this is about you and me. It

147

is about you, and where you will spend eternity. Come with us, and I promise, you will know the peace a life with Jesus can bring. Stay here, and you will be tormented by God's judgment."

"We're in a battle, Thomas. Joshua ben-David and all the armies of the world against a pathetic god no one can see and the only two men in the world stupid enough to defend him. I'm on the winning side, Thomas. So you just go back to your little hideaway in the mountains, and we'll see who comes out on top."

"Come on, Anthony, let's go."

"He's not going anywhere," Carolyn said and grabbed our son's arm.

I would have made a scene, but Habib placed a stern hand on my shoulder and in a voice that was barely audible said, "It is his choice, my friend."

Anthony seemed genuinely torn. He looked to me and then to his mother and back. Then firm resolution set his jaw. He looked at Carolyn and said, "Ma, I believe in what Pop's done. I'm going with him."

"No way, young man. You're gonna stay right here with me."

Anthony broke his arm free. "I'm not your little boy anymore. This is my life we're talkin' about here. And I'm not gonna throw it away just to stay here with you. I don't believe the king is a god."

"Tony!"

"If he was a god, why did he have to bring us here to try and catch Pop? I ain't never followin' a man like that. I—I'm sorry, Ma."

With that, the three of us walked toward the door to the sound of Carolyn shouting and kicking, trying to rouse the guards.

We could not have picked a better time to leave the city. It was almost time for the evening worship service to begin. The recently empty streets were now filled with shuffling, moaning people all going to the Temple to bow at the feet of Joshua ben-David and to hear him rail against the God of James and John. The Sons of Thunder would doubtless be there as well, perhaps to call down a new curse on the unrepentant or to remind ben-David just how little time he had left. I was sorry I would have to miss it.

The immediate benefit for us was that all the king's horses and all the king's men would not be able to locate the three figures that blended in so well with the masses. Habib had enough foresight to bring two extra cloaks for Carolyn and Anthony. As we walked, I thought about what a pity it was that only one was being used.

Habib drove so I could talk to my son. Anthony told me about how rough things had gotten in New York since the Black Knight impact. People had panicked en masse, and looting and rioting became everyday occurrences. Carolyn was still at work one day when two men broke into her apartment. Anthony was alone but was able to chase them away with a baseball bat and a few strong swings.

And then there was the news from overseas: the Sons of Thunder. At first, they were an academic curiosity, and people in New York were no more interested in them than they were the next local political race. Until the day New York Harbor turned to blood.

That was when Anthony began to take notice. He watched the news every day as well as many of my live reports from Jerusalem, even though some of those happened in the wee hours of the morning, New York time. He said that he had been nearly ready to accept Jesus as Messiah for quite a while, but that he needed the final push from someone he knew who also believed. He was glad I was that person.

Back at Petra, we were given a hero's welcome. Patma and Miri had organized a huge dinner in our honor, and one hundred fifty people crowded into the living area of Habib's cave. Most stood for lack of space to sit. Normal conversation from that many people in such a confined space would have been loud, but these people were joyful and louder than normal. I barely heard Habib's announcement that the food was ready.

Before dinner began, I wanted to introduce Anthony to his new spiritual family. "Everyone, listen," I said above the din. The voices quieted. "I want to introduce someone to you. This young man comes to us all the way from New York City. He has sacrificed everything and everyone he holds dear to follow Messiah Yeshua. He and I have had some rough times in the past, but we have determined to let the past stay there. He is my son, but I realized today that he is no longer a child. Ladies and Gentlemen, Brothers and Sisters in the Lord—"

"Excuse me, but may I finish?"

Stunned, I stared at Anthony and stepped back, gesturing with open hands to let him know he had the floor. Had that formal request come from my son from Brooklyn? What happened to the accent?

"My father can be a bit long-winded." He smiled as the guests chuckled. "What he was trying to tell you is that my name is Anthony. Anthony Ian Beckett. And I am pleased to meet all of you."

149

Epilogue

It has been over three years since I penned those last words. I am amazed that I have not even had the desire to put pen to paper and record the many exciting things that have been happening. I could say that I have been too busy, but that explanation would be inadequate. The truth is that God has turned my priorities upside-down. I care more for people now than I do events. No longer an observer, I am an active servant of my God and King, Yeshua of Nazareth.

So, having said that, why am I writing now? I write now out of sheer anticipation. Messiah will return in a matter of days. Even now, the armies of mankind are gathering themselves for their final challenge against the army of God. But I am getting ahead of myself. Perhaps I should begin the day the last prophecy was fulfilled.

Rabbi Dyan had asked our techno-guru, Sam Isaacs, to use his scavenged electronic equipment to set up a viewing room in one of the caves. Satellite reception had not been good since the debris from Black Knight made a home in the stratosphere, but Sam agreed to do his best, knowing better than to question the rabbi.

At noon on the appointed day, several hundred of us gathered in the largest of the caves, where a projection screen had been set up. Sam had mounted speakers outside the cave, so that nearly all the inhabitants of Petra would be able to at least hear what the rabbi apparently knew would happen on the news.

I stood near the screen, between Rabbi Dyan and Anthony. I remembered from my tutoring sessions the significance of this day. I whispered to Rabbi Dyan, "Is today what I think it is?"

"Just watch," he said, not taking his eyes off the screen.

An enfeebled and diseased Linda Friedman stood outside the courtyard of Joshua ben-David's palace. James and John were preaching just outside the gate. Hundreds of soldiers poured into the courtyard and flooded the streets, hopelessly surrounding the prophets. The Sons of Thunder seemed to not even notice. Their attention was focussed on the figure of a man looking down from a second story balcony. Joshua ben-David gripped the railing and stood silent, stiff, and tall.

The soldiers moved into position and stood ready for their next order.

James and John shouted at the king. "Listen to us, Son of dust," said James. "Today is the final chance you will have to repent before the full wrath of God falls on you and your followers. Our ministry is ended, but do not be arrogant. Your power lasts only seventy-five more days."

Ben-David raised his right hand. Dozens of rifle barrels pointed toward the two robed men.

James and John raised their hands above their heads in unison, turned their faces to the sky and smiled.

The king dropped his hand. Smoke filled the palace courtyard as hundreds of bullets pummeled the bodies of the Sons of Thunder.

The death of James and John was not half as outrageous as the reaction from Joshua ben-David's followers worldwide. It was a global Mardi Gras. The cursed, sun-scorched, boil-infected masses were ecstatic to finally be rid of the two men they believed were responsible for their misery.

How hopelessly human of them to feel that way. We are often all too eager to place the blame for our pain and suffering anywhere but where it rightfully belongs—on ourselves.

In fact, the world was so happy to see the Sons of Thunder lying dead on the palace steps that the king forbade burial. Instead, he had them dragged to the street just outside the palace courtyard, where the people would have free access to the bodies and the king could still see them from his window.

For a full three days following the execution, Jerusalem was consumed in a macabre celebration. Sick, disfigured forms danced night and day around the bloody corpses. Bands played in the streets. And revelers defiled the bodies in every way their diseased minds could imagine while the major networks carried full coverage.

The images were revolting, but I greeted each of those days with increasing anticipation. The prophecy in Revelation is clear. The two witnesses will lie in the street for three and a half days, at which time God will raise them up and take them away. And that day was approaching like a train in the distance. I heard the whistle a little louder every morning.

Rabbi Dyan organized a covert mission for anyone who wanted to go to Jerusalem on that fourth day to watch the two men of God stand up and ascend into heaven. I was one of the first volunteers, right behind Anthony.

"You know this will be nothing more than a dangerous sight-seeing tour," I said to him. "Are you sure you want to risk it?"

He grinned. "What, are you joking? I wouldn't miss this for the world."

I shared his excitement. Up until that time, we had seen many amazing things, both good and bad. Anthony and I had seen God deliver us from Joshua ben-David's men time and again, but the chance to stand within feet of a Biblical miracle as it happened was just too tempting for caution. In our desire to be a part of something that special, my son and I were just alike.

I cannot resist the swelling pride I feel each time I think of my son. He has quickly developed into a leader of men. He is focussed, secure, and confident. Would you believe me if I said I always knew he had it within himself to be that kind of man? Probably not. Well, no matter. God knew Anthony had strong leadership abilities, and He is using Habib and others to develop those qualities.

Our expedition was limited to ten. They were Rabbi Dyan, Habib, Miri, Anthony, myself, and five others from the various scouting parties. Nearly three hundred volunteered, but we collectively decided that, for this party at least, more was not merrier.

We ten donned the now-familiar disguises and made our way to Jerusalem. Upon entering the city, I decided that we did not need disguises after all. No one was sober enough to notice us. Had we worn kilts and bagpipes, we would have obtained the same reaction from Jerusalem's citizenry. That is to say, none.

The scene in the palace courtyard was even more shocking in person than it was on television. The air reeked of urine and feces and vomit. Without a word, the ten of us moved upwind of the bodies.

A boil-scarred woman danced naked in a figure eight around the fallen prophets as four men savagely kicked, spat on, and cursed their lifeless forms.

And on the same balcony from which he had decreed their demise stood Joshua ben-David, smiling.

We were definitely out of our element. How can the family of God enjoy hell's party? Habib suggested we break up into groups of twos and threes and spread out a bit to avoid drawing attention to ourselves. Anthony and Miri stayed with me, while Rabbi Dyan and Habib ambled off to our left.

A heavily inebriated old man stumbled into Miri and said something to her in Arabic. He evidently wanted to know why she was not celebrating with everyone else, because she answered his challenge with a silly little jig that made us all laugh. Satisfied, the old man went about his business.

Anthony pointed at the sky and said, "Look!"

The dirty gray sky had a golden hole in it. The hole grew to twice its original size before the naked woman screamed.

James and John stood, cleansed of human filth and blood, clothed in a shaft of blinding light that emanated from the hole in the sky. People scurried, crawled, and ran like roaches in the light from the now-living men. The general shock had barely taken hold when a voice like thunder drowned out all screams.

It said, "Come."

At that, James and John began to rise to meet the light as if on an invisible elevator. I wanted to wave, to yell, to somehow get their attention so they would know believers were there to share in their miracle and to bid them bon voyage. But I restrained myself, seeing on their faces nothing of earth, only heaven.

They saw Jesus, and no one down here could possibly interest them more.

I think our feet touched more air than soil on the return trip to Petra. Our comrades who watched everything on television were just as joyful as we ten adventurers. It was our turn to celebrate, and celebrate we did.

Even as the armies of the world exchange the first volleys of destruction on the field of Meggido, songs of praise, adoration, and victory rise and fall all over Petra. For a short time, the world celebrated the meager victories of Joshua ben-David, but we now revel in the <u>final</u> victory of Messiah Yeshua as we eagerly await His entrance.

THE END

A Final Word from the Author

Dear Reader:

You may be like Thomas Beckett, someone who does not believe in "religion." But I want you to know that this is not a book about religion. It is about the truth. And the truth is that Jesus of Nazareth is the Son of God, and He is coming soon to judge the world. Just like Thomas, you have a choice to make. Will you give your heart to the Lord now, believing that He loves you and wants the best for you, or will you wait until it is too late?

The blood Jesus shed two thousand years ago sealed an everlasting covenant between God and anyone who will receive His forgiveness. Any one of us is free to take part in that covenant until the day Messiah Jesus returns to judge the world.

The clock is ticking. Time is running out.

Today is the day of salvation (2Cor 6:2). Open up your heart to Him and pray this prayer right now:

> "Lord Jesus, I come to You just as I am, a sinner. I know I can't be good enough on my own to please You. That's why You had to suffer and die, to be my sin offering. Your blood sealed the covenant that I can now have with God the Father. I ask You to forgive me of my sin. Cleanse me of all unrighteousness. Come into my heart and be my righteousness. Thank You, Jesus, for forgiving my sins, and thank You, Father God, for the blood covenant I now have with You through Your Son Jesus."

If you prayed that prayer with sincerity and conviction, then you are saved. You are a new creation, according to Second Corinthians 5:17.

Now, forget that person you used to be and live the rest of your days as the new person God has made you. He has changed you on the inside. You are in right standing with Him. Begin to cooperate with Him as he works to complete that change, conforming you to the image of His Son.

I hope that the Lord has been able to use this novel to touch your life. God bless.